THE WORLD FAMOUS
HOTEL ROYALE

↰ totally where I live!

DRAMAS
OF A TEENAGE
A
HEIRESS

KATY BIRCHALL

EGMONT

EGMONT

We bring stories to life

First published in Great Britain 2018
by Egmont UK Limited
The Yellow Building, 1 Nicholas Road, London W11 4AN

Text copyright © 2018 Katy Birchall

The moral rights of the author have been asserted

ISBN 978 1 4052 8651 0

67131/001

A CIP catalogue record for this title is available
from the British Library

Typeset by Avon DataSet Ltd, Bidford on Avon, Warwickshire
Printed and bound in Great Britain by the CPI Group

Stay safe online. Any website addresses listed in this book are correct
at the time of going to print. However, Egmont is not responsible for
content hosted by third parties. Please be aware that online content
can be subject to change and websites can contain content that is
unsuitable for children. We advise that all children are supervised
when using the internet.

Egmont takes its responsibility to the planet and its inhabitants very
seriously. All the papers we use are from well-managed forests run by
responsible suppliers.

For Sam, Luke and Lily

THE WORLD FAMOUS
HOTEL ROYALE

DRAMAS
OF A TEENAGE
HEIRESS

Also by Katy Birchall

Hotel Royale series
Secrets of a Teenage Heiress

It Girl series
Superstar Geek
Team Awkward
Don't Tell the Bridesmaid

THE DAILY POST

TEENAGE HEIRESS IN SHOCK HANDBAG SCANDAL!

By Nancy Rose

I've met celebrities with colossal egos before. But it is not every day that I, Nancy Rose, *Daily Post* columnist, am WRESTLED TO THE GROUND by a celebrity, before being assaulted by her FEROCIOUS SAUSAGE DOG. And all for a one-of-a-kind handbag. But I can EXCLUSIVELY REVEAL that yesterday evening Felicity Royale and her dog Fritz did just that.

Attending fashion designer Lewis Blume's launch for his new collection, I innocently reached for a handbag on display, a one-off with silhouettes of dachshunds across the front. How lovely, I thought as I admired the stitching. I love dogs and all animals. I'm so pleased I often donate to animal charities.

Before you read on, please be aware that what happened next may DISTRESS READERS.

In a completely unprovoked attack, I was TACKLED to the ground by none other than the teenage heiress to Hotel Royale, who insisted that the bag was hers!

Sending shockwaves through the other guests, Miss Royale's WILD dachshund then ATTEMPTED TO BITE ME as the heiress continued to claw the bag from my hands.

Although the main incident was missed by the cameras, footage of Miss Royale then being ESCORTED OUT BY SECURITY is currently circulating online.

I would like to assure my fans that I am recovering well and, to those who were already aware of the incident, thank you for all your kind messages of support.

For my full reaction, check out today's YouTube vlog at NancyRose and don't forget to subscribe for all the juiciest celeb gossip and daily dramas!

ONE

My life is over.

I had decided never to emerge from underneath my duvet again, and my plan was working perfectly until my mum came barging into my room – which STILL doesn't have a lock on it, despite all my requests, because Mum seems to think she has the right to just barrel on in and invade my privacy whenever she likes.

'Don't you think you're being a little dramatic?' she said with a sigh, yanking the duvet off me.

Fritz, my dachshund, immediately hopped down from the bed, where he'd been snoozing comfortably next to me, and began pawing at her leg until she scooped him up in her arms and tickled his belly.

You know, considering I feed him every day, I'd expect a little more loyalty.

'I am NOT being dramatic,' I huffed, narrowing my eyes at the traitorous Fritz and pulling the duvet back over myself. 'But while you're here, can you pass me a pen and paper? I need to write up my last will and testament. If you bring me breakfast in bed, I promise to leave you my extensive collection of moisturisers. And I know Grace has her eye on those so you'd better act fast.'

Mum rolled her eyes and put Fritz down into his basket. 'It is not *that* bad.'

'It is EXACTLY that bad,' I whined, ducking my head back under the duvet and curling up into a ball beneath it. 'It is MORTIFYING. My life is ruined. No one will want to be my friend. I'll be exiled from society just like that Romeo guy in that Shakespeare play.'

'When did you read *Romeo and Juliet?*' Mum asked, sounding impressed and a little bit too surprised for my liking.

'That is *not* important right now!' I declared, in my most superior tone.

I also decided to brush over the fact that I hadn't *exactly* read the play, but I was totally listening when my best friend Grace was talking about it with her brother Olly the other day.

Well, half listening. I got distracted a few minutes into their debate by a video on my phone of all these jumping goats.

They really were very funny.

'Mum,' I said, bringing the conversation back to the practical issues at hand. 'We should consider moving country. I've had a look online, and there are some very tempting options. Did you know that New Zealand is home to the world's most diverse penguin population? I know, right? Sounds like a cool place to live, if you ask me.'

'Flick, we're not moving to New Zealand and you're not writing your will. Instead, you can talk me through what happened last night. That is, if you're ready to talk about the incident.'

'I will NEVER be ready to talk about it. And anyway, you already know what happened. It's EVERYWHERE online.'

'I know Nancy Rose's version of what happened, but I'm more interested in yours.'

'What's the point?' I groaned. 'No one is going to believe me.'

'I'll believe you.'

I peered over the top of the duvet suspiciously.

'Fine,' I said with another world-weary sigh, and then I launched into EXACTLY what happened, no exaggerations . . .

★ ❀ ☽

The famous designer Lewis Blume had invited Fritz and

me to the launch of his new handbag collection. Only people who had been living under a rock in the Outer Hebrides wouldn't have heard that we were very special guests of Lewis's because one of the pieces in his new collection just so happens to be The Fritz – a handbag inspired by my amazing, trendsetting dachshund.

Which should come as no surprise because Fritz is a total superstar these days. His Instagram is off the charts, and he's way more in demand than all those French bulldogs wearing hats and stuff. Fritz was voted the most stylish dog by *Tatler* AND he's even getting his very own calendar next year.

So, when we got the call saying he was Lewis Blume's latest muse, I was like, DUH, of course he is.

And I made sure he looked his very best for the launch, in his favourite Ralph Lauren tuxedo complete with silk polka-dot pocket square, and his new collar, specially designed by British supermodel and dog-lover David Gandy, who delivered it personally to Fritz last week.

To be honest, Fritz may have looked good and his bag was AMAZING, but I was kind of bored at the launch because, even though I was surrounded by cool celebrities, I hardly knew anyone there. My pop-star friend, Skylar Chase, was selfishly still in LA and my vlogger pal, Ethan

Duke, had to go to some stupid teen awards instead. So I stood looking around, and that's when I saw her. Nancy Rose. Standing by The Fritz handbag. Rubbing her hands together and reaching out for it with her talon-like nails, crying, 'Mwahahahaha, this bag SHALL BE MINE! FOREVER MI—'

★ ❀ ଚ

'Ahem.'

'What?' I exclaimed, cut off in mid flow.

'I thought you said no exaggerations.'

'I'm not exaggerating, *Mother.*'

She raised her eyebrows. 'You're telling me that Nancy Rose was standing in front of The Fritz handbag, cackling and yelling, "This bag shall be mine!" in the middle of a launch?'

'OK, FINE, that was a slight exaggeration.' I sighed. 'Can I continue with the story now?'

'Please do.'

★ ❀ ଚ

ANYWAY, that's when I saw her. Nancy Rose. Standing by The Fritz handbag. Rubbing her hands together and then reaching out for it with her talon-like nails. And while she might not have cried, 'Mwahahahaha, this bag SHALL BE MINE! FOREVER MINE!', she *did* flutter her eyelashes at Lewis Blume, who happened to be standing nearby, and said something along the lines of, 'This exact bag would be *perfect* for an event I'm attending tomorrow.'

Which may sound innocent, but there was no way I was going to let Nancy Rose take that bag for a stupid event she's attending for the following reasons:

1.   That bag on display was a ONE-OFF piece, with a special embroidered message to Fritz on the inside.

2.   If anyone was going to be photographed FIRST holding that handbag, it was going to be FRITZ, who inspired it in the first place.

3.   And if it was perhaps a little too big for Fritz to carry, then it was going to be ME.

4.   And if it wasn't me, then maybe the Queen or Beyoncé or someone.

5.   Whoever it was, it was NOT going to be gossip-columnist Nancy Rose who has, in the past, said some very mean things on her stupid vlog about my very good friend Skylar Chase.

Holding Fritz, I casually sauntered over to where Nancy Rose was standing next to the bag, and I forced myself to be open-minded about her, even though I overheard her telling someone nearby that she thinks animals (thus including beautiful innocent sausage dogs like Fritz) are VERMIN and when she has taken over 10 Downing Street with her evil plan, she's going to destroy all —

★ ❀ ೨

'Ahem.'

'WHAT?' I demanded, throwing a pillow at Mum as she attempted to hide a smile.

'The exaggerating thing,' she explained. 'You're doing it again.'

'You know what, Mum, you're really obstructing my whole vibe.'

'Go from the bit where you walk up to Nancy Rose,' she said, 'and no embellishments this time.'

'You have no flair for good storytelling,' I said, sighing.

★ ❀ ೨

SO, I walked up to Nancy Rose, with Fritz under my arm,

and she was talking to someone about boring, non-evil, standard stuff, blah blah blah.

'Flick Royale,' she said as she noticed me, offering me her hand to shake. 'I don't think we've ever met. I'm Nancy Rose. I was just admiring this handbag – inspired by your dog, I believe.'

'I overheard,' I replied through gritted teeth, but shook her hand very politely because I have IMPECCABLE manners.

'I was actually hoping to borrow it for this event I'm going to tomorrow. It's for a dog charity and I —'

'Actually, I was hoping to have it for an event FRITZ is going to tomorrow,' I said quickly. 'But Fritz is very glad you like it.'

'Excuse me?'

And that's when she smiled at me, this *really* fake smile through her bright red lipstick as though she had stumbled upon something juicy for her column.

'I *said* Fritz is very glad you like it.'

'Before that, you said you would be using the bag tomorrow? Forgive me, but isn't that up to the designer?' she said, tilting her head as though talking to a baby. 'Lewis often lends me first-off-the-line items for his collection, so that I can display them on my vlog, and I wouldn't bother showing any item that has already been photographed on someone else. I don't do sloppy seconds.' She sniffed. 'Especially after . . . a dog.'

Fritz growled.

'Fritz's bag will be available for anyone to buy, it's just that this particular handbag here on display was made especially for him because of the inscription,' I explained, patiently. 'I can show you if you —'

'I don't know if you know, *Felicity*, but my vlog is really very popular, so the things designers lend me get a lot of views and I doubt Lewis will want to miss that opportunity.' She paused before doing that thin-lipped smile again. 'Tell me, Flick, does Lewis Blume give you items for your vlog?'

Then she picked up the handbag and let it hang daintily from her wrist, as though modelling it to the room.

Which is when I kind of exploded. Because that comment about the vlog may have sounded fine to an innocent bystander BUT it was in fact a very pointed thing to say, because Nancy Rose knows full well that my vlog, launched earlier this year, hasn't exactly had the attention I hoped it would.

So, I did what *anyone* would do in that situation and I snatched the handbag from her and put it on my own wrist. Where it belongs. Next to Fritz.

And you know what? She snatched it right back

from me. Which was VERY childish.

I obviously had to reach out and grab the handle to take it back again.

Next thing I knew, I was having a tug of war with Nancy Rose over The Fritz handbag and everyone was staring and gasping, and Fritz started barking because he didn't want her to ruin his special handbag with her pointy talons, AND THEN Nancy Rose LET GO of her side of the handle, causing her to go flying backwards.

Seriously, hasn't she ever played tug of war before?

That's how she ended up on the floor. It was her own stupid fault for not holding on to the bag properly. I did NOT tackle her. And Fritz didn't go anywhere near her. He would never bite anyone.

Which is exactly what I told the security man, Jeremy, as he led me out of the party. And Jeremy nodded along and offered me a Fruit Pastille while I waited for my driver, which I politely declined because I had no idea how long the packet had been in his pocket and it looked a bit squished.

But still, it was a nice thing for him to do and you could tell he was totally on my side.

I paused to take a deep breath.

'I see.' Mum nodded.

'That is the full story. Mum, we have to leave the country,' I pleaded, burying my face in my pillow. 'Thanks to Nancy Rose's version of what happened last night, everyone is saying mean things about me.'

'Not everyone. Prince Gustav Xavier III tweeted this morning, saying that you are a very nice young lady with exceptional selfie-stick skills and he can't imagine that a word of her story is true.'

'Wait.' I poked my head out the duvet. 'Prince Gustav is on *Twitter* now? I thought he was still getting to grips with Instagram.'

I remembered all too well the painful incident of having to watch the European socialite prince attempt to use my selfie stick for his first Instagram post (which I'd witnessed from inside his wardrobe, because I was trying to steal the selfie stick back from him . . . but that's another story). Thankfully, since then he's started dating Skylar Chase and not only has the wardrobe incident been forgotten but also he's got better at taking photos. He's even been experimenting with filters.

'He must be building his brand.' Mum shrugged.

'You know, Mum, I was considering apologising to Nancy Rose. I woke up this morning feeling a bit guilty about the way I acted.' I pursed my lips. 'But then I saw her vlog and now I'm NEVER apologising.'

'Yes, I don't exactly agree with how she's gone about things, but —'

'There was a fleeting moment when I thought that this whole thing might boost my vlog's popularity. Any publicity is good publicity kind of thing. But do you know what?'

Mum looked at me blankly. 'What?'

'I checked my subscribers this morning and the numbers have gone DOWN.'

Mum didn't exactly look distressed by this new information. She'd never wanted me to have a vlog. She had banned me ages ago from having a YouTube channel until Cal, the son of her most trusted employee, head concierge Matthew, and someone I had known since we were little, had persuaded her it would be a good thing for me to do.

I don't know why she trusts Cal's word over mine. Although he is quite smart and he never gets into trouble at school, whereas I've already had detention twice this term: once for stealthily answering my phone in assembly (it was Sky calling from LA, what was I meant to do? *Ignore* her? She's won a Grammy. You do NOT ignore people who have won Grammys); and the second for missing an entire maths lesson because Grace spilled ketchup on my purse and I had to pop home to the hotel and ask Amy in housekeeping how I could get it out before it stained. Which, if you ask me, is a perfectly good reason to miss out on a few sums but whatever.

Still, I'm just as responsible as Cal. I proved it too last term when Mum grounded me FOREVER after I hid in Prince Gustav's wardrobe in his hotel room. And then she grounded me again because I sneaked out one night with Sky to attend a fashion show when I was supposed to be doing my homework. That was the end of my social life for a while. Stuck here in the hotel, I spent the whole time helping everyone out, tagging along with all the different teams and learning the ropes, which was all excellent research for my vlog.

But it turns out it's not that easy to gain followers on YouTube and now, thanks to Nancy Rose, everyone thinks I'm awful. There's no chance people will want to hear a word I have to say.

'How many hits has her vlog about me got now?' I asked Mum. 'You can refresh the page on my laptop.'

Mum turned to my desk, on which my laptop was sitting already open on Nancy Rose's YouTube channel. She leaned over and clicked the refresh button.

'Well?' I sniffed, watching her. 'How many?'

She examined the screen and then straightened, looking shocked.

'Uh . . .' She hesitated, before shutting my laptop firmly. 'It doesn't say.'

I groaned and slumped back on to my pillows. Mum was a terrible liar.

'Flick, don't let this get you down. We do, however, need to have a serious talk about your behaviour at the launch, but we can leave that until later.'

'Can't wait.'

'And don't worry about Nancy Rose's silly vlog. By this evening, everyone will have forgotten about it.'

By the evening, the 'silly vlog' had gone viral and a mass of paparazzi had gathered outside the hotel.

I know this sounds crazy, but I think I actually prefer it when I'm wrong and Mum is right.

✦ ✿ ೨

Flick, are you OK?
I keep trying to call

Sorry, Grace, I'm kind of in hiding today

I completely understand
That vlog is so mean! Clearly just lies.
Cal, Olly and I all agree that Nancy
Rose is the WORST. Is there
anything we can do?

Nothing. Thanks, though

You want us to come over
and cheer you up? We don't
have to talk about what happened

I'd rather be on my own for now.
I'll see you guys at school.
Thanks for being the best friend
ever, though

BTW, I've come up with a plan

A plan? For what?

It's genius

What are you talking about?
What plan?

A plan to take down Nancy Rose.
Want to hear it?

Um. OK

We lure her to a deserted warehouse

That's a creepy start

We wait in the shadows for her to arrive

Getting weirder

And then when we've got her right
where we want her . . .

I regret asking
about this plan

WE THROW WATER BALLOONS AT HER
MWAHAHAHAHAHAHAHAHAHAHAHA

Wait. THAT'S IT?! Water balloons? That's your genius plan?

I know, right! It's so great. It's got it all: mystery, suspense, a climactic water balloon attack! What do you think?

Uh . . . how long have you been working on this plan?

Since I saw the video, so six hours ago! I've done a tactical breakdown diagram of everyone's positions and everything. Why?

Grace, you won a school award for academic achievement

Yeah?

You're top of every single class. You're the brightest person I know

??

19

And you've spent six hours coming up with a plan . . . to throw water balloons

What's your point??

Never mind. I'll call tomorrow

I'll keep working on the genius plan. What are your thoughts on Super Soakers? Is that making things too complicated??

Night Grace xxx

TWO

By the time I got to school on Monday, I was ready for the day to be over. I never should have left my bed but Mum forced me to get up, giving me an unwelcome lecture at the same time all about proving to the haters that I'm not afraid of them.

Firstly, when did Mum start thinking she could pull off phrases like 'the haters' and secondly, I am one hundred per cent afraid of them.

'Chin up,' she said as I bade Fritz goodbye and we got in our private lift from our flat on the fifteenth floor. She pushed the button for reception. 'Don't let Nancy Rose win.'

'Her video has now gone viral and she's even uploaded a second one to talk about her "brush with death" at my hands,' I said with a sigh. 'I think she's already won, Mum.'

The doors pinged open and we stepped out into the main lobby. Even though I've lived at Hotel Royale all my life, I never get tired of the view when the lift doors open on to reception. My great-great-grandfather, who founded the hotel yonks ago, wanted it to be the grandest hotel in the world, so he made sure it had all these big columns and sparkling chandeliers and marble floors, then he shoved a load of gold leafing all over the plush wallpaper just in case it wasn't obvious that this place was super posh. I like to think that my great-great-grandfather was a total drama queen who kept saying things like, 'More gold, people, *give me more gold*!'

In my head for some reason he also has a French accent.

'Good morning,' Matthew said cheerily, shooting me a big grin as he came out from behind reception. 'And how are we today?'

'I hate my life.'

'Excellent! Ready to smash that Monday morning!'

He winked at Mum. 'Christine, Audrey was looking for you. She wants to run through your 9 a.m. meeting notes.'

I don't know how Matthew is so jolly all the time. As head concierge, he has to talk to every guest and be super nice to them, even if they're mean or grumpy, and he has to sort out all their yawn-inducing problems. Plus, he heads up the hotel's booking system, which is the most boring spreadsheet in the world and he's been doing it for YEARS. Last year, I was in charge of the spreadsheet for just one day and I was bored out of my mind.

Somehow, he thinks he has the best job in the world.

'I could never work anywhere but Hotel Royale,' he once said to me with this twinkle in his eye. 'It is magical.'

Which, you know, is sweet and everything, but I also kind of threw up in my mouth.

'Thank you, Matthew,' Mum said. 'Is Audrey in her office?'

'I'm here!'

Audrey's voice echoed through reception accompanied by the familiar sound of her unbelievably high stilettos clacking across the marble floor. I know I should be amazed by how organised and important she is, being general manager of the hotel, but I genuinely think I'm more impressed by Audrey's ability to walk around in those stilettos. I actually saw her run in them once, when she was 'late' for an important appointment and I swear, she looked just like those giraffes galloping through the plains on David Attenborough documentaries. Also, Audrey is NEVER late to anything but she always thinks she is, which means when she takes me anywhere we're always a hundred years early.

When I mentioned her giraffe-gallop, though, she didn't look very impressed. Whatever – they're elegant creatures. Better than the comparison she made about me that time I borrowed some roses from reception and put them in my room for a party (because technically the hotel is MY house so by default they're MY flowers). Audrey gave me this funny look when she found out and said I reminded her a bit of Edmund from the Narnia books. I googled him and that is NOT a compliment. He betrays his family for some Turkish delight, which is the worst.

I mean, what kind of moron chooses gross Turkish delight? If you're going to go to all that trouble betraying people, at least let it be for something good, like cola bottles or a Dip Dab.

'Are you available for a quick chat before our meeting, Christine?' Audrey said, juggling some files in her arms.

'I'm just going to put Flick in a car to school and then we can —'

'Mum, I can walk to school.'

'Not with them you can't,' she said firmly, nodding towards the crowd of photographers and journalists milling around outside the front steps.

Seriously, how do I have all this attention and yet NO ONE IS SUBSCRIBING TO MY VLOG?

Matthew organised a driver to pick me up from the side entrance, but the reporters weren't fooled. Thanks to the constant flow of celebrities and high-profile guests staying at the Royale all year round, the paparazzi know the hotel layout pretty well and they've learned all our tricks. Some of them were covering the side entrance and as soon as I stepped out into the street towards the car, we were bombarded with questions and camera lenses.

'Flick, why did you attack Nancy Rose?'

'Do you have any comments about the incident?'

'Flick, how do you feel about her comment this morning that you aren't worthy of being the heiress to Hotel Royale?'

'Flick, do you consider yourself a diva?'

'Flick, did you attack Nancy Rose for attention?'

'Would you describe yourself as a wild child?'

Mum slammed the door firmly behind me as I scrambled into the back seat and the driver, Peter, put his foot down. I let out a long sigh and buried my head in my hands as we pulled away. When I looked up I could see Peter glancing at me with concern in the rear-view mirror. Sky once told me never to listen to the questions and rumours that the reporters yell at you; she said they're just looking for a reaction they can play on. But one question was still ringing through my ears as we arrived at the school gates.

'Flick, how do you feel about her comment this morning that you aren't worthy of being the heiress to Hotel Royale?'

'That's ridiculous,' Cal said, after I found him waiting by my locker with Grace and Olly, and had filled them all in about Nancy Rose's new declaration. 'Of course you're *worthy* of being the heiress to Hotel Royale.'

'What does that even mean anyway?' Olly added, rolling his eyes.

'It means that respected heiresses shouldn't be horrible brats and attack journalists. Not that I did,' I replied, opening my locker.

I yelped as all my books came exploding out at me, scattering across the floor.

'When are you going to tidy your locker?' Olly laughed as the three of them bent down to help me pick everything up. 'This happens every day.'

'This does not happen *every* day,' I protested. Olly and Cal shared a smirk as Grace helped me battle my books back into my locker and slam the door shut before they could fall out again.

Since the events of last term, I'd been hanging out with Grace, her brother Olly, and Cal a lot more and we'd become a sort of oddball friendship group. I'd only got to know Grace and Olly last year, but Cal I'd known forever. We used to be best friends when we were little and got into loads of trouble around the hotel, but then he turned into a big nerd who always wore headphones round his neck like they were an accessory and only talked about things like books and Star Trek, so, in his words, I had swiftly 'dropped him like a hot potato'.

Which is such a nerd way to put it. No one uses the phrase 'hot potato' any more.

Anyway, the three of them were very low maintenance compared to Ella, who I had a big fall out with last term.

It was nice having friends who weren't using you for popularity points or free backstage passes. The more I thought about it, the less I could remember why Ella and I had been friends in the first place. It's not like we ever had real fun or laughed together until our stomachs ached (this happens with Grace on an almost daily basis. Her teacher impressions are second to none). Ella had loved complaining about everything, making snide remarks about other people in our year, and only really cared about *looking* like she was having fun rather than actually having any. We spent our whole time making sure everyone knew we were the elite of the school.

Then, last term, she saw me waiting tables at the hotel and spread all these rumours about me, saying that I had been lying all the time about hanging out with celebrities and being best friends with Skylar Chase.

Which was only partly true. Technically I had told a couple of white lies about the people I'd hung out with at the hotel BUT becoming friends with Sky was a hundred per cent true. Anyway, Grace told her off for saying mean things about me to everyone and then Grace's brother Olly broke up with Ella because she wasn't being very nice and also because she kept pulling out his arm hair when she fawned all over him.

Ella totally blames me for both those things and never talks to me now. I tried to make amends at Christmas, before the start of the new term, but she wasn't interested. She takes every chance she can to throw me a dirty look and then say something under her breath to whichever one of her adoring minions is standing next to her. You'd think she'd cut me some slack considering the number of outfits I've let her borrow over the years.

'You don't really listen to anything Nancy Rose says, do you?' Cal asked. 'She's just annoyed with you because you attacked her. It will blow over and she'll find someone else to torture.'

'Just to reiterate, I did NOT attack her. She took Fritz's bag and then I simply *reminded* her that it didn't belong to her. She's blown this whole thing out of proportion and made me sound like a diva. Which I'm absolutely not, as you know!'

I turned to the others for reassurance. None of them were looking me in the eye.

'I'm *not* a diva,' I said, in case they hadn't heard the first time. 'As you know. Right?'

'Sure. Right.' Olly nodded.

'Absolutely not,' Grace said.

'So down to earth,' Cal added seriously.

And then the three of them started sniggering. WHO ARE THESE TRAITORS I CALL MY FRIENDS?

'Hey! I'm not a diva!' I cried in exasperation.

'Although up until recently you did have that diva strut going on.' Cal grinned. 'And there was that time you demanded the Hotel Royale chef make Fritz a three-tiered caked for his half birthday . . .'

'I wanted Fritz to feel special!' I protested. 'And I did not demand it. I asked Chef Kian if he had time to —'

'And the time she refused to walk to the shop, and made Peter drive her,' Olly pointed out, nodding along with Cal.

'OK, that is so NOT what happened. It was raining that day and Peter offered to drive me when he saw me setting off with all my bags and —'

'Don't forget the time she made us microwave her ice cream,' Grace chimed in gleefully.

'That ice cream was FREEZING!' I crossed my

arms grumpily. 'I can't believe this. I'm having the worst time because of Nancy Rose and now my own friends are attacking me for —'

Cal held up his hands, interrupting me. 'Flick, calm down, we're messing with you!'

'Of course we know you're not a diva!' Grace giggled.

Just as I opened my mouth to speak, someone bumped my shoulder from behind, making me stumble forwards into Cal who had to steady me. I turned round to see Ella smirking.

'*Sorry*, Flick,' she said, not sounding sorry at all. 'Didn't see you there.'

'No problem,' I said through gritted teeth.

'I *really* enjoyed Nancy Rose's new vlog.'

'Move along, Ella,' Olly said quickly, looking at her in disgust.

Ella blushed, the harsh words from her ex-boyfriend clearly stinging, but not enough for her to leave us alone.

'I wasn't surprised to hear about what happened between you and her,' she continued smugly. 'You should really learn how to control your fiery temper.'

'I do NOT have a fiery temper,' I snapped irritably.

Because I have auburn hair, I get teased a lot about being a hothead, which just makes me MORE of a hothead.

'You see?' She gasped, looking taken aback. 'Here I

am just trying to be nice and you're throwing it back in my face! Just like with Nancy Rose. No wonder she's calling you a diva. You've *really* changed.'

My cheeks flushed with anger and I felt Cal's hand press gently on the back of my arm in warning. I could hear his voice in my head telling me not to rise to it.

'I haven't changed, Ella,' I seethed. 'I've just come to learn who my real friends are.'

'Well, do they know who *you* really are?'

'What's that supposed to mean?' I asked, glaring at her.

'Hello, am I the only one who watched Nancy Rose's vlog?' she asked, with a baffled expression. 'Flick attacked her over a handbag! Who does that?'

'That is not what happened. I didn't —'

'No smoke without fire, Flick. And I've seen the footage of you being escorted out of the room by security, so you must have done *something*.' She tossed her hair back before turning to Cal and saying, 'Cal, I'm surprised that you in particular aren't angrier at your *friend*. Don't you want to be a journalist some day?'

'Well, yeah,' Cal mumbled, seeming stunned that she even knew who he was. 'But that doesn't mean —'

'If Flick hadn't let her temper get the better of her, maybe she would have thought twice about launching an attack on someone who would have been an amazing contact for you. Nancy Rose is one of the most famous journalists in the world.'

'OK, for the LAST TIME, I did not attack —'

'But then, I guess you are a really nice guy.' She smiled sweetly at him, before giving me a pointed look. 'Maybe that should be a little more appreciated by your friend Flick here.'

My jaw fell to the floor.

'Anyway,' she said smugly, 'I had better go get my seat in assembly. Just remember, Flick, that your selfish behaviour reflects badly on everyone around you. Something to keep in mind.'

I could feel a strange kind of rage bubbling and twisting through my stomach as she turned on her heel and sauntered down the corridor.

THREE

On the way to assembly, it dawned on me what Ella was up to.

It was SO obvious. She couldn't bear that Grace and Olly picked me over her last term, so now she was jumping on the Nancy Rose bandwagon, trying to make all my friends think I'm a terrible person and turn them against me!

It made perfect sense. She had been wanting to get back at me ever since our falling out last term and Nancy Rose had given her the perfect opportunity.

'Think about it, Grace,' I said under my breath as we made our way to assembly, the boys walking ahead of us. 'Why else would she tell Cal that he was a nice guy?'

'It was a bit strange,' Grace agreed. 'The last time she spoke to Cal it was to tell him that his hair reminded her of an erratically blow-dried poodle.'

'She is out to get me and you HAVE to be on your guard to make sure that she doesn't turn you against me with her snide remarks. It's all part of her cunning plan.'

Grace laughed. 'Don't be silly, Flick! You know what Ella's like, she just says stupid things. We know to ignore her. But I wouldn't worry, I don't think she's concocted some genius plan to make all your friends dislike you.'

'You don't know Ella like I do,' I huffed. 'She can hold a grudge. Did I ever tell you about the time I drank her coconut water?'

'Um, no?'

'Boy, was that a drama.' I sighed, recalling the incident. 'I thought she wouldn't mind if I drank her coconut water, but it turned out it wasn't just any coconut water, it was *special* coconut water that her mum had had imported for her, and that was the last carton. To this day, I wish I had never touched it.'

Grace blinked at me. 'What happened?'

'She was so angry that she uninvited me from a sleepover at her house.'

'She uninvited you from a sleepover because you drank her *coconut water*?' Grace looked stunned. 'You're joking, right?'

'Sadly not,' I said, as we took our seats in the main hall. 'I had to ask Matthew if he could work his head concierge magic and track some down for me.'

'And did he?'

'You know his motto, Grace.' I smiled. '*Anything is*

34

possible at Hotel Royale. He managed to get a whole crate sent in. After I showed up at school with that for her, she bought me a new friendship bracelet.'

'Wow.' Grace nodded, looking impressed. 'All that because of some coconut water.'

'I'm telling you, Grace,' I whispered, spotting Ella a few rows ahead chatting to some girls in the year above, 'this morning was probably just the beginning. She's probably talking about me right now to those girls. Probably telling them that I'm the worst person in the world and not to go anywhere near me.'

Grace and I both leaned forwards to try and listen in to her conversation.

'I think,' Grace began thoughtfully, 'she's actually talking about perfume.'

'Of course! Don't you get it?' I hissed, shaking my head at Ella's back. 'Perfume is floral! Floral, like *roses*! Like Nancy ROSE! She's tapping into everybody's subconscious, laying the groundwork so that everyone is thinking about it all the time!'

Grace gave me a strange look and opened her mouth to speak, but then the headmistress, Mrs Walker, arrived and the room descended into hush.

Mrs Walker began reading out the various notices but I couldn't listen; I was too distracted by the back of Ella's head. I kept thinking about what she'd said to Cal before assembly and every time I thought about it, I felt a new wave of anger.

She had always been jealous of me, even while we were friends. I remembered how pleased she was when she came for lunch at the hotel with her mum. She caught me serving guests their food because Timothy, one of our best waiters, was teaching me how everything in the dining room works. She had been so quick to spread rumours about me. And even now, when we hadn't spoken for weeks, she was straight in there, jumping for joy at my public humiliation. Had she ever been my friend at all? Or had she always been lying in wait, secretly hoping that I would screw up? Ugh, I felt so betrayed!

Ella is SO Edmund with the Turkish delight.

I was so engrossed in Ella's backstabbing that I didn't hear Mrs Walker call out Cal's name.

'What's Cal doing?' I whispered to Grace as he stood up and went to the front of the hall.

'You'll see,' she said with a smile.

Cal cleared his throat and he shuffled his feet nervously as the entire school waited for him to speak.

'I would like to announce that we are launching a school newspaper, which will report on school news and events, as well as including interesting general features and competitions. Uh . . . we will be holding our first meeting after school today for anyone who would like to join the editorial team, and the first issue will be published at the end of term. Yeah. Thanks.'

He scuffled hurriedly back to his seat and Mrs Walker thanked him, emphasising that the newspaper would be an excellent opportunity for budding journalists and would look good on university and job applications.

'Why didn't he tell me?' I asked Grace who gave him a thumbs up when he caught her eye.

'You had a lot on your mind,' she explained before adding proudly, 'I'm going to be an investigative reporter.'

'I thought you wanted to be a vet when you were older?' I whispered in confusion.

'It's good to have a range of activities and interests on your applications. Veterinary courses are competitive; I have to stand out. It's not all about grades.'

I sat back in my seat as Mrs Walker read out the rest of the notices, before dismissing everyone for the first lesson of the day. I didn't get the chance to ask Cal about the whole newspaper thing, so I had to wait until lunchtime when we were sitting in our now-usual corner of the canteen.

Every room I'd walked into since the start of the day had descended into ripples of whispers, so I wasn't exactly surprised that all the students in the canteen looked up as I came in and then watched me sit down.

'Do they all seriously believe that I tackled Nancy Rose to the ground over a handbag?' I sighed, glancing nervously around me.

'I think it's a good thing,' Grace said cheerily.

'How is it a good thing?' I asked, baffled.

'No one will mess with you now. I think most people are genuinely impressed that you took someone down.'

'I did not take someone down,' I groaned, lowering my fork and burying my head in my hands. 'She tried to take the handbag from me.'

'Technically, you took it from her first,' Cal added.

I glared at him. 'Whose side are you on?'

'Always yours,' he replied with a mischievous grin. 'Even if you are a bit of a diva.'

'Like Grace said, I think being escorted out of a handbag launch will do wonders for your street cred.' Olly nodded, taking a sip of water. 'No one will ever consider taking a dachshund handbag from you again.'

'Let's change the subject,' I insisted, wishing I could go home and hide under my duvet again. 'So, a school newspaper, huh, Cal? You should have said something.'

'I felt you might not be too fond of journalists at the moment.'

'*Some* journalists,' I replied.

'I can't wait to get started on the paper,' Olly said enthusiastically. 'I've got some great ideas for the first issue.'

'Wait a second . . .' I looked from Olly to Cal and back to Olly again. 'You're involved in the newspaper too?'

'Meet the brand-new political commentator and film critic.' Olly smiled. 'It's an unusual combination, I know.'

'Wow,' I said. I knew Olly wanted to go into politics or be a lawyer, despite his musical talents, so it kind of made sense.

'I'm hoping that having someone as popular as Olly on the team might boost the appeal of joining,' Cal said knowingly. 'When word gets out that you're involved, the crowds will flock.'

'Ew.' Grace wrinkled her nose as her brother laughed off Cal's comments.

Cal was probably right, though. Olly was one of the hottest boys in the school, with his long dark eyelashes and sharp cheekbones and everything. Sometimes, when we talk, I find it hard to concentrate on what he's saying because his eyes are so pretty and I get all lost in them and then I realise that he's asked me a question and is waiting for a reply. I usually have no idea what he's asked me because I've been thinking about how intense his eyes are, and whether he uses an eyelash curler or if that can possibly be natural, so I panic and just have to nod and go, 'YES,' confidently, hoping for the best.

This has led to many an awkward situation, like the time I accidentally agreed to be a backing singer with Grace at one of his band's gigs.

Three minutes into the first rehearsal, he stopped the song, turned round to me with this amused expression and said, 'I thought you said you could sing?'

Which is precisely why I did NOT leave my state-of-the-art speakers to Olly in my will that I wrote the other day after watching Nancy Rose's vlog, despite him always whining on about how badly he wants the same ones. That will teach him for being so rude about my angelic vocals.

Instead, those beauties will be going to Bruce, Grace's tortoise.

'So, the team is looking strong so far,' Cal continued. 'We have Olly on culture, Grace as our lead investigative reporter and I will be heading up general features.'

'And you're the editor,' Grace said, making Cal blush. 'Kind of an important role.'

'I'm hoping we'll get some keen photographers too. Olly, doesn't your friend Liam have a pretty cool camera?'

Before Olly could answer, I cleared my throat.

'What about me?'

The three of them blinked back at me.

'What about you?' Cal asked, looking confused.

'What's my role?'

'You . . . you want a role on the paper?' Cal shared a confused glance with Olly. 'You realise it would be extra work. You know, outside of school. You'd have to come up with ideas and stuff.'

'What's that supposed to mean?' I said huffily, narrowing my eyes at him.

'Nothing, nothing.' Cal laughed, holding up his hands. 'Don't want to rile the Handbag Hooligan.'

'I am NOT a Handbag Hooligan,' I fumed, feeling my cheeks growing hot. 'And for your information there are loads of ideas I can bring to your stupid newspaper. Loads.'

'Like?' He said, leaning back and folding his arms with a bemused expression.

Honestly, there is no one in the world who can wind me up and get under my skin like Cal Weston can. He loves doing it too, which makes it even MORE infuriating.

'Like . . . well . . .' My mind went blank. 'I'll . . . think of something, just you see.'

'I look forward to hearing your pitch at the first meeting after school.' Cal grinned. 'See you there?'

'Oh, you bet you will.'

Later on I kind of regretted my decision. I had exactly *zero* ideas to bring to the paper and I didn't know how I could be of any help, either. Everyone else had their specific interests, and working on this paper would help their future career. My future career was already decided for me – running Hotel Royale – and the only other interest I could think of that I had was my dog and his, frankly, fabulous wardrobe.

So, I decided that I would just tell Cal that actually, he was right. I didn't have anything to bring to his stupid newspaper. I had plenty of other pressing things to do with my very important time, thank you very much.

Like trying to convince the world that I wasn't a Handbag Hooligan.

When the bell rang, I marched determinedly into the classroom where the newspaper meeting was being held and straight up to Cal who was standing by the board at the front.

'Cal,' I announced, before he could say anything. 'I'm not here to help —'

'Then why are you here?' a bored voice asked from the corner of the room.

I turned round and my jaw dropped.

'Meet the newest member of our team,' Cal said, shooting a warning look as he gestured to Ella.

You have GOT to be kidding.

FOUR

'What was I supposed to do, tell her she couldn't join because you don't like her?'

'YES!'

Cal rolled his eyes from the seat next to me as Peter brought the car to a halt at some traffic lights. Reporters had been gathering around the school since lunchtime, hoping to catch me on my way out, so Mum had made sure Peter was there to drive me back. Cal usually just mills about the hotel after school, waiting for his dad to finish work, so I selflessly offered him a lift to the Royale with me after the newspaper meeting, with absolutely no hidden agenda, just out of the kindness of my heart.

But if he didn't agree to cut Ella from his newspaper team, then he could walk home.

'That's not how it works, Flick.'

'She's trying to make you all think I'm a horrible person! She's never even spoken to you before and now suddenly she wants to be your best friend!'

'She doesn't want to be my best friend; she wants to

do fashion pages for the paper. She's trying to get an internship at a fashion magazine, so this would look good on her CV.' Cal sighed. 'She didn't say anything about you in the meeting before you arrived.'

'Cal, I'm telling you, I don't trust her. Why else would she volunteer to work on *your* newspaper?'

'I don't know, Flick,' Cal said, looking hurt. '*Maybe* she doesn't have a secret plot and just *maybe* she thinks me launching a newspaper is actually a really good idea.'

'You know I didn't mean . . . Cal, I think the newspaper is a *great* idea. But I'm supposed to be your friend.'

Cal looked taken aback. 'You *are* my friend.'

'Not if Ella has anything to do with it! Didn't you hear what she said this morning? According to her, I'm bad news for your future!'

Cal shook his head. 'If you think that I would ever let someone like Ella make me think badly of you —'

'She's determined to show everyone that Nancy Rose is right about me.' I looked down at my hands. 'And you already think I'm a bit of a diva.'

'Oh, come on,' Cal said, sounding exasperated. 'We were joking about that stuff! We love that —'

'I don't understand why you've let her join your team. Now you're going to be spending all your time with her.'

'Flick, do you think that maybe you're overreacting

slightly?' Cal raised his eyebrows. 'Since Nancy Rose's vlog went up, you've seen Ella twice and have decided that she's out to get you.'

'Because I know what she's like. What about the coconut water?'

'What?' Cal looked baffled. 'Why are you talking about coconut —'

Peter cleared his throat loudly. 'Sorry to interrupt but we're home.'

The car door suddenly swung open on my side and I looked up at Matthew and one of the doormen, who had both battled their way through the paparazzi and were waiting to guide us back up the main steps. While Cal was still undoing his seat belt, I thanked Peter in my most gracious, un-diva-like voice and then jumped out of the car and under the doorman's protective arm before Cal could say anything else.

Fritz was waiting for me on one of the purple velvet chairs in the lobby. When he saw me come round the heavy swivel doors, he jumped down and scrabbled across the marble floor eagerly.

'Hey, boy.' I laughed, scooping him up in my arms and letting him lick my chin. 'Are you ready for your next Instagram post?'

I plonked him on top of reception and immediately

got a telling off from Matthew as he came in, shielding Cal from the paparazzi.

'You know Audrey's rule, he's not allowed up here,' he scolded, tucking his hands under Fritz's belly and passing him back to me. He quickly got out a dust cloth and began squeaking it across the surface. 'No paw marks on reception please.'

I plopped Fritz back down on the floor and let him rush around reception back to the door to greet Cal.

'Your son is being very irritating,' I told Matthew, while he finished polishing the desk and then began to polish the gold buttons on his dark green uniform. I don't think I've ever seen Matthew with a hair out of place.

'You two had a scrap again, have you?' He laughed.

'Flick's annoyed because she hasn't got her way,' Cal informed him, rolling his eyes and tickling Fritz behind the ears which made Fritz's tongue loll out happily.

'That's not true! It's the principle!' I snapped. 'You know how upset I am about what happened with Nancy Rose and now *this* just makes it all ten times worse!'

'Oh, I wouldn't take any notice, Flick,' Matthew said, straightening his jacket. 'Nobody bothers to read those lists anyway.'

Cal and I exchanged a confused glance.

'What list?'

47

Matthew's eyes grew wide. 'Oh! Nothing! Sorry, I thought you were . . . talking about something else. Don't mind me, carry on!'

'We were talking about Ella joining the school newspaper,' Cal said. 'What were *you* talking about?'

'Matthew, what list?' I asked again.

'I . . . maybe you should . . .' he began, flustered, but was saved by Audrey emerging from her office, typing into her phone.

'How was school?' she asked brightly, spotting me and Cal. Then she noticed Matthew's face. 'What's wrong?'

'What's this about a list?' I asked, putting my hands on my hips.

'Oh.' Audrey put her phone down. 'You haven't seen it.'

'Seen what?' Cal asked.

'It's a load of rubbish,' Audrey said, sighing. 'So don't get upset.'

'Okaaaaay? Can someone PLEASE just tell me what's going on?' I insisted.

Audrey nodded and typed something into her phone before holding the screen up for me to see. It was a tweet sent by Nancy Rose about an hour earlier.

@NancyRose
BREAKING: @FlickRoyale DROPPED from '50 Heirs

to Watch' list due to be published tomorrow! Source close to heiress told me EXCLUSIVELY, 'It's time everyone knew the REAL Flick Royale.'

Audrey and Matthew watched me with expressions of concern as I read the tweet several times.

'Are you OK?' Audrey asked carefully as I handed her phone back.

'They dropped me from the top fifty? But I've been forty-nine for years!'

'You are number one in our eyes no matter what,' Matthew said firmly. 'And nobody even reads those—'

'It's been retweeted thousands of times,' I said, feeling numb.

I took out my own phone and went on to Twitter, turning my notifications back on. After receiving nasty comments about the handbag vlog from plenty of strangers, I'd muted my social media for the day. I had completely missed all of this.

My phone immediately started vibrating as all the comments, retweets and likes came flowing in, thanks to Nancy Rose tagging me in her original tweet.

'Block her,' Cal instructed me sternly. 'And don't read anything else.'

'Who gave her that quote? What "source" close to

49

me?' I shook my head. 'What does that even mean, the "real" Flick Royale? It sounds like I'm pretending to be someone I'm not.'

'She'll have made all that nonsense up to get more clicks,' Audrey said angrily. 'No one you know would ever speak to Nancy Rose.'

'Wait a minute,' I said, switching from my notifications to my general newsfeed of people I follow. 'Cal, look who just retweeted it.'

I held up my screen so that he could see. He didn't say anything as I pointed at Ella's name.

'No one I know would ever speak to Nancy Rose, isn't that what you just said, Audrey?' I muttered, staring at Ella's profile picture. 'I wouldn't be too sure about that.'

And then I walked away to the lift, leaving them all in silence.

Hey, are you ok???

OMG SKY! No, not ok. It's so good to hear from you. Want to Skype?

I would love to but I'm just in the middle of a photo shoot. Isn't it like 1am in London?

Couldn't sleep. I got dropped from the 50 Heirs to Watch list

You were on that list?? Cool! Oh. Sorry. I mean, who cares about some weird list? Not me

This is all Nancy Rose's fault

Did you really tackle her to the floor? Can't say I feel bad for her. She once likened my outfit to a 'Christmas tree, if a dog had been left alone to tear it apart'.

I didn't tackle her to the floor. I wouldn't even know HOW to tackle someone to the floor

She made the whole thing up then? Why?!

51

Well, I did take the handbag from her. But she stole it from Fritz first, so it was only fair

Sounds dramatic!

It was a little dramatic. Everyone hates me now

That's not true

Yes, it is. How can I prove to everyone that I'm not a nasty diva person?

You don't need to prove ANYTHING! Your friends and family know the real you and that's all that matters!

According to the 50 Heirs to Watch list, the 'real me' doesn't deserve to be on it

You're not REALLY upset about that list, are you? I get dropped from lists all the time. It doesn't mean anything

That was the only list I was on! I was so proud to be number 49!

Can I do anything to make you feel better?

Leave LA and come to London?

Soon. You know it's my new favourite place. Ah I gotta go, they want me to change into the Dior. Ignore the haters and ignore all of Nancy Rose's tweets. You're the BEST. Love ya xxx

Wait.

What do you mean ignore ALL of Nancy Rose's tweets?!

She only tweeted one thing about me, right?!

I blocked her so I only saw that earlier tweet about the list!

What has she said now???

I'm going to look

No I shouldn't

I shouldn't look

Should I?

Why would I torture myself?

I won't look

Although, what if people are talking about it and I can't defend myself because I don't know what she's tweeting?!

> I'm going to look

> I'm looking right now

> DON'T TRY TO STOP ME

> ...

> Oh god

> This is not good

@NancyRose

Excited to be on the Morning Sunshine *breakfast show tomorrow, revealing all about HANDBAG GATE and an EXCLUSIVE story about Flick Royale's previous ATTACK ON ROYALTY! #handbaggate*

FIVE

One of the best things about living in a hotel is the kitchen.

Cal and I used to hang out in the Hotel Royale kitchen all the time, mostly to play hilarious pranks on Chef Kian who is, by the way, the best person on the planet to wind up. We always used to steal his chef's hat and give it to random tourists on the street, which used to drive him NUTS, and once we snuck in to the kitchen in the middle of the night when Cal was staying over, stole every single wooden spoon there was from the drawers, and hid them in various places around the hotel. We left him clues to their whereabouts and everything, so it was like his own special treasure hunt.

We were literally woken up in the early hours by his roars of frustration and it took him days to find the one in the main reception vase. Cal and I managed to persuade a group of tourists that it was a famous art installation by Andy Warhol, named 'The Wooden Spoon Amongst the Flowers'.

We got in so much trouble but it was totally worth it.

I don't play many pranks on Chef any more, but I do enjoy going down to the kitchen after school to snaffle some leftover treats from the pastry chefs or offer Chef my invaluable opinion on the new pudding he's added to the menu that week. The kitchen is especially helpful when I've had a bad day and need a comforting sanctuary. Cal and I have both agreed that there is no problem that Chef's chocolate mousse can't solve.

And discovering you've sparked a trending hashtag is DEFINITELY a problem. So even though it was the early hours of the morning, I decided I would go and enter the sanctuary of the kitchen, rather than lying in bed, trying and failing to sleep.

I pulled off my duvet and slid out of bed, reaching for my dressing gown and slippers. Fritz heard me and immediately opened his eyes, jumping out of his bed, which was next to mine, and taking a long stretch.

'It's not morning yet, Fritz,' I explained, as he wagged his tail ready for his walk. 'Go back to sleep.'

But he wouldn't stop pawing at my leg, and when I plonked him back into his bed, he just hopped right out of it again. Giving up, I found his fluffy white personalised dressing gown neatly folded in his drawer, and wrapped it round him snugly so he wouldn't be cold, before lifting him under my arm and heading out of my room. Sneaking across the floor, I carefully unlocked the flat door and shuffled through into the hallway, pressing the button for our lift.

Hotel Royale is always open for business, as Matthew proudly likes to remind anyone who will listen. 'Since we opened, and even during the wars,' he says, in this wise voice as though he's letting you in on this big secret, 'the Royale has never shut its doors. Not once.'

I told him that, technically, the Royale DID shut its doors that time I burnt a pizza in the flat and it activated all the fire alarms and everyone had to evacuate to wait for the fire brigade to arrive and sort it out.

He got all tight-lipped after that and Audrey made me apologise later that day for ruining his moment.

Boys are so weird.

Anyway, the hotel is open right through the night, so when my lift doors opened into the lobby at 2 a.m., the night receptionist, Erin, was there, welcoming a guest who had just arrived after a long day travelling. She spotted me as I plodded across the polished floor in the direction of the kitchen.

'Flick?' she said suddenly, having got one of the night porters to help the guest with his bags. She stepped out from behind reception and walked towards me, looking suspicious. 'It's very late. What are you up to?'

'Late-night snack.' I shrugged. 'Or early morning, if you will.'

She tilted her head. 'With Fritz?'

'Oh yeah, right.' I sighed.

I'd completely forgotten about Chef's stupid no-dogs-in-the-kitchen rule. I'd told Chef a hundred times that Fritz is the most hygienic dog in the world because, *hello*, I bath him several times a week, plus this really posh Covent Garden spa sent me a special 'Pampered Pooch' collection, so he is very well groomed. Just ask his Instagram fans; the picture of him with his ears flapping about in the air as he was having a blow-dry is one of his biggest hits.

But Chef refused to budge and just went, all pompously, 'A dog is a dog is a dog.'

Which literally means nothing.

Erin held out her arms. 'I'll look after him until you're done.'

'Thanks,' I said gratefully, passing him over. He immediately began licking her chin and she giggled. Fritz is one of the biggest flirts I've ever met.

'Flick, are you OK?' Erin asked gently. 'The handbag thing with Nancy Rose and everything . . .' She trailed off.

'I'm fine,' I replied, embarrassed.

'You should know that everyone on the team is certain

that, whatever happened, there's no way she's telling the full truth.' She smiled warmly.

'Thanks, Erin,' I said, opening the door leading down to the kitchen. 'And thanks for taking care of Fritz. I'll be back in a second.'

I hurried through the door before she could say anything else. On reaching the kitchen, I instinctively went towards the baking cupboard, which is where Chef keeps all his cake decorations, including chocolate buttons of all different sizes. I peered into the cupboard, careful not to let the door close behind me and shut me in like last time, and nabbed a bag of buttons from the shelf. Just as I was about to dig in, a voice spoke behind me.

'Flick.'

Now, it might be fair to say that I mildly overreacted to this voice coming out of the darkness of the kitchen but, in my defence, there's the matter of Colin Whittle.

Last year, when I was trying to impress my mum by learning all about the history of the hotel, I came across the story of Colin Whittle, who was one of its original builders in the 1900s. He freaked out because he kept seeing this ghost come out at him from the walls, so he started protesting about the hotel being built at all. Ever since I read about Colin Whittle and his spooky sightings, I've been keeping an eye out for any strange occurrences, just in case.

I recently thought that the hotel ghost was behind my missing trainers and tried for days to convince Audrey to arrange a séance, but it turned out they were just under my jumper I'd left on the floor.

But, still, the Colin Whittle story was lodged in my brain, so when I heard someone say my name just as I began to help myself to some chocolate buttons, I jumped about five metres in the air, sending the entire packet of buttons flying upwards, and screamed so loudly that my throat stayed sore for hours.

'It's OK, it's just me!' Mum cried, her hands clamped over her ears.

'What are you doing?!' I hissed. 'Now look what you've done. Chocolate buttons everywhere. Chef is going to kill you.

'Oh, this is *my* fault, is it?' Mum raised her eyebrows as she gestured to the buttons scattered across the floor.

'Yes! Why did you sneak up on me?'

'I didn't mean to sneak up on you. What are you doing in the kitchen at this time?'

'I wanted chocolate buttons.'

'At two in the morning?'

'I couldn't sleep.' I narrowed my eyes at her. 'Were you following me?'

'No, no,' she said, all innocently, 'I just wanted chocolate buttons too.'

Mum leaned back against the surface, watching me as I went to the cleaning cupboard to fish out a dustpan and brush. Mum never wore pyjamas, in case any of the hotel staff ever needed her urgently during the night and she had to just get up and go, so she was wearing a blue cashmere jumper and linen trousers. The only thing that gave away the fact that she'd been sleeping was her unbrushed hair. Somehow, though, it still looked quite neat by normal standards. Mum constantly looked as though she was going to a very important meeting.

I crouched down and started sweeping up the chocolate buttons, but after about a minute I let out a long sigh and turned to her.

'What?' I said stubbornly.

'What do you mean, "what"?'

'You're giving me that look.'

'No, I'm not.'

'Yes, you are. It's your worried look. I can feel it burning into the back of my head.'

She smiled. 'That obvious, huh?'

'To be fair, it's better than your impatient look, which I'm much more used to. Kind of nice to see your face mixed up a little bit.'

'Matthew and Audrey told me about the "50 Heirs to Watch" list.'

'Did they also tell you Nancy Rose is appearing on *Morning Sunshine* tomorrow to talk about handbag-gate?'

She tried to stifle a laugh.

'Mum, it's not funny!'

'I know, I know,' she said, still chuckling. 'It's just the term "handbag-gate". It is a *little* funny.'

'Well, it's definitely not funny that she's revealing an exclusive story about me attacking royalty.'

Mum's expression turned more serious. 'No, I guess not.'

'She's talking about me hiding in Prince Gustav Xavier III's wardrobe last year when I was trying to get my selfie stick back, isn't she? That has to be it.' I shook my head. 'How can she possibly know about that?'

'I don't know,' Mum said with a shrug. 'People talk. It must have found its way to her somehow. At least you know that Prince Gustav is a friend of yours and will make sure everyone knows the truth.'

'That hardly matters.'

She looked at me curiously. 'What do you mean?'

'Mum, the truth is that I *did* hide in his wardrobe last year and almost give him a heart attack when his security team discovered me in there.'

'Yes, but—'

'So, what does it matter if Prince Gustav and I are now friends? Nancy Rose is just going to twist it into backing up her story about handbag-gate. No one will believe anything I say.'

I poured the chocolate buttons into the bin, put away the dustpan and brush, and leaned on the kitchen surface next to her.

'I think the source who told her about the Prince Gustav incident is the same person who told her everyone is going to see the "real me",' I said confidently. 'What does that mean? If there is a *real* me, what's the *fake* me?'

'It's just nonsense. You can't let it get to you,' Mum said, wrapping an arm round my shoulders. 'You have to rise above it.'

'How can I rise above it when *everyone* is talking about it? I don't want people to think I'm a horrible person who doesn't deserve to be on the "50 Heirs to Watch" list.'

Mum looked thoughtful for a moment. 'Did I ever tell you that I was on that list once upon a time?'

'You were?'

'Oh yes. You are looking at the former number twenty-seven.'

'Wow!' I was stunned. 'Are you serious? That's way better than forty-nine!'

'I was quite a bit older than you are now. But then the following year I was dropped from the list completely and never made it on there again. You know why?'

I shook my head.

'I'd spent the year turning down invitations to fashionable events because I was busy learning the ropes from your grandfather about managing this place.' She smiled, looking around her. 'And I'd say I've done an all right job, wouldn't you?'

'The best! So,' I said slowly, 'your point is that the list was wrong about you?'

'You bet it was.' She grinned. 'Now, I don't think Chef would notice if we opened another bag of chocolate buttons, do you? We can always blame Matthew.'

As Mum went to fish some more buttons out of the baking cupboard, I mulled over what she'd just said. Just like Mum, I had to prove to everyone that they'd got the wrong idea about me. The *real* me.

All I had to do was work out how.

SIX

Did you hear that?!

Hear what?! WAS IT THE PUMA???

WHAT? What are you talking about? What puma?!

The escaped puma

There's an ESCAPED PUMA?

Yes! It escaped from its owner and was last sighted in the London area. Isn't it exciting?!

NO, A PUMA ON THE LOOSE IS NOT EXCITING, GRACE

Flick, don't worry. They rarely attack humans. Only if they mistake you for prey

Well, now I feel MUCH better

So, that wasn't it?

Wasn't what?

What you heard just now? You didn't hear the "meow" of the escaped puma?

No, I didn't hear a MEOW of an escaped puma

What did you hear then?

I was talking about Ella's comment!

Oh. What comment?

When she put up her hand just now!

Oh. Right. Yes, I did hear that.

Want to try and find the puma tonight?

He must be feeling so scared in the city!

He's probably very hungry. Let's buy some tuna.

Cats like tuna, right? Even big cats?

STOP TALKING ABOUT THE PUMA.

Ella's comment was so snide about me!

I can't believe you didn't notice!

Her comment about
Pride and Prejudice??

YES!!

I'm lost

She just said that everyone in the book
THINKS Mr Wickham is nice
but that true colours always show
themselves one way or another!!

Riiiiiiiiiiiiiiiiiiiight?

SHE'S CLEARLY TALKING
ABOUT ME

What?? Are you sure??

Of course!! She is saying
that I am Mr Wickham!!

Huh?

Just like Mr Wickham showed his
true colours by running off with Lydia,
I have shown MY true colours through
handbag-gate!!

What true colours?

That's my POINT. Ella thinks
that everyone should see me
as the HANDBAG HOOLIGAN!

You know, I quite like the name
Handbag Hooligan.
It's catchy

Grace, FOCUS please

I don't know, Flick, I think she was just making a comment about Mr Wickham. I don't think it was about handbag-gate

Did you watch Morning Sunshine?

Yes, and Olly and I both agreed it could have been a lot worse

How comforting

I think Nancy Rose's story about you and Prince Gustav was HILARIOUS! I love the idea of you holding his PA ransom using a water pistol until Prince Gustav returned your selfie stick! Way more entertaining than what really happened

Do you know what someone said today as I passed them in the corridor?

What?

They went, 'some people are so selfish.'

How do you know they were talking about you?

It was clearly about handbag-gate! How can I make it all stop?!

It's only because they've heard one side of the story, because, you know, she's got a popular vlog and everything. But popularity does not equal accuracy!

Grace. That's it. You're a GENIUS

Nah, I think I read that popularity saying on that quote-a-day toilet paper so I can't take credit

Not about that. About the popular vlog!

Uh-oh

No, don't be worried, I'll
come up with the perfect plan

Not that. I think Mr Hampton knows we are
messaging under the table. He just
raised his eyebrow at me

Don't be paranoid. He has no idea.
Teachers are so STUPID. Hahahaha

DETENTION SIGN-IN
WEDNESDAY 24th JANUARY

NAME	TEACHER/ CLASS	REASON FOR DETENTION
Tom Ferris	Mr Grindle/ Study period in library	Caught drawing Mr Grindle with the body of an ostrich
Liam Bailey	Mr Grindle/ Study period in library	Caught drawing Mr Grindle with the body of a flamingo
Grace Dillon	Mr Hampton/ English	Texting during class
Flick Royale	Mr Hampton/ English	Texting during class and, when phone was confiscated, accusing Mr Hampton of displaying "handbag-gate bias"

SEVEN

I decided to call Ethan Duke.

Grace gave me the idea when she said that thing about Nancy Rose having the platform of her popular vlog. If I had the same kind of platform, I could PROVE to everyone I was a nice person and not a Handbag Hooligan! It was perfect!

The only problem was that my channel didn't exactly have the same kind of following that Nancy Rose's did. A picture of my sausage dog dressed in a cowboy outfit got WAY more hits than all of my vlogs combined. BUT what I could do is show everyone the 'real me', or whatever, *via* someone with a vlog as popular as Nancy Rose's.

Someone like Ethan Duke, one of the biggest YouTube stars on the planet. Everyone listens to him.

I hadn't seen Ethan since the Hotel Royale Christmas Ball when he'd been my date, but it turned out that he saw me as just a friend and that actually he was completely in love with his model friend Jacob who, by the way, also attended the ball, but on the arm of someone else.

Despite the fact that Ethan Duke is the perfect specimen with these really full lips, strong eyebrows and a jawline that my mum embarrassingly described as 'truly majestic', I got over the situation pretty quick. Anyway, we were still friends and he had always said I should be a guest on his YouTube channel, we just hadn't got round to it yet. If ever there was a time to call in a favour from Ethan Duke, it was now.

There was no time to lose.

I asked Mr Grindle, who was in charge of detention, if I could pop out and make a VERY important phone call, but he just peered over his book at me and said all sarcastically, 'Yes, I'm sure it's a matter of life and death.'

I told him that yes, in fact it WAS a matter of life and death, because in case he hadn't noticed, I happened to be a national disgrace, thanks to Nancy Rose and handbag-gate, and if I didn't make this phone call, my life was well and truly over.

But he was all grumpy about it and didn't budge, forcing me to wait until after detention was over. Mr Grindle has never been my biggest fan, largely because I do an excellent impression of his weird ostrich walk and also maybe because of the time I told him that if he wanted to get ahead in the dating game at his age, he should consider trimming his nose hair.

As soon as I got out of the school gates and into Peter's car – which was actually unnecessary because, thanks to my being held back at school an hour, the reporters had all assumed I'd given them the slip and left – I called Ethan's number and waited nervously for him to answer.

'Flick!' he said warmly down the phone. 'Long time, no speak. How are you?'

I was relieved that he sounded pleased to hear from me. Even though we were technically friends, he was still super famous and busy, so I wasn't sure if he'd bother picking up.

'Ethan, I'm sorry to call you like this, but I need a massive favour.'

'What can I do?'

'I need your help to change my image.'

'Like a makeover?' He sounded confused.

'No, no. Not my physical image. My image in the eyes of the nation.'

'Is this because of handbag-gate?'

'Yes. I need to show everyone who I really am. Thanks to Nancy Rose and the footage of me being escorted from Lewis's launch, I don't exactly have a huge fan base right now.'

'OK, so you want me to interview you on my vlog or

something? Get your side of the story?'

'No.' I took a deep breath. 'I had something a little more creative in mind. Are you free this evening by any chance?'

'Actually, you caught me on the rare night I have nothing to do. I can be at the hotel in about half an hour. Will that work?'

★ ❀ ∂

As soon as I got home from school, I went through my entire wardrobe and picked out the most sophisticated clothes I could find – black skinny jeans, a black polo neck, a long beige trench coat and strappy high heels, completing the look with bright red lipstick.

'What would you think if you saw me, Fritz?' I asked him, checking my reflection as he chewed on one of Mum's shoes. *'There goes a Handbag Hooligan? Or, There goes a nice person who should be on the "50 Heirs to Watch" list?'*

Fritz barked loudly, before getting back to his chewing.

'That's the answer I was hoping for.' I laughed, getting his lead ready to take him down with me. 'We have to prove to everyone that you're a good boy too, who would never bite anyone, so you're coming along with me.'

Ethan was waiting for us at reception when I came

down in the lift and when he saw me coming across the lobby, he broke into a wide grin. Taking in his perfect jawline, I was reminded of the time I first met him, when I literally could not stop saying 'JAW'.

'Wow,' he said, walking over to give me a hug. 'You look great.'

'Thanks jaw . . . I mean, Ethan!'

Seriously. WHAT IS WRONG WITH ME?

'Anyway,' I said hurriedly, hoping he hadn't noticed my slip up, 'do you think the outfit is too much?'

'Never. It looks good.'

He bent down to fuss Fritz, who I had purposefully dressed in the knitted jumper Ethan had given him for Christmas. It said MODEL BEHAVIOUR on the back.

'So, what's this plan you've got up your sleeve, then?' Ethan asked, laughing as Fritz licked his jaw all over. I'm clearly not the only one who appreciates it.

'I want you to live-stream us hanging out,' I said excitedly. 'Just like you sometimes do with other guests on your vlog.'

'OK, sounds good,' he said, before gesturing to my backpack. 'What have you got in there?'

'I'm not going to tell you because it's a surprise.'

He raised his eyebrows. 'Right. And you're sure about this?'

'Absolutely. Why wouldn't I be?'

'Sometimes a response can fuel the flames, that's all,' he said carefully. 'Nancy Rose isn't likely to play nice. I just want to make sure you definitely want to go ahead with this, whatever you're planning on doing.'

'This isn't a response to Nancy Rose, Ethan,' I said smugly. 'I'm just appearing on your vlog, and if it so happens that your vlog shows the REAL me and contradicts everything people think about me because of handbag-gate, then that's just a happy coincidence.'

He grinned. 'All right, you're the boss. So, how do you want to start?'

'First, you need to tweet that you're about to live-stream to your feeds with me as your special guest. Make sure you tag me and no harm in tagging some media people, you know, like *Morning Sunshine*, for example.'

He got out his phone and began typing into it, before showing me the tweet ready to go.

@EthanDuke
NEW VLOG ALERT: live-streaming NOW with my good friend @FlickRoyale. It's going to be a laugh, check it out!

'Tell me when to press send.'

'I think we should start in the hotel, because it's pretty, and then we're going to head over to the park,' I instructed.

'OK,' he said, getting his phone ready to live-stream. 'And we'll just chat normally. I can ask you some questions about growing up here, that kind of thing. An insight into Flick Royale's life, basically. Is that what you want?'

'Perfect. I'm ready when you are.'

I straightened Fritz's jumper and then checked my hair.

'Just be as natural as possible,' Ethan directed. 'Think of it as just having a conversation with me, as though the camera's not there. Do you want to do a practise run of a few questions first, so you get used to my phone pointing at you?'

'No, it's OK,' I said confidently. 'It will get dark soon, so we can just go straight into it.'

'All right, then.' He smiled. 'I'm going to press send on that tweet.'

I gave him a thumbs up. *Here goes nothing*.

'Sent! And we're . . . live!'

EIGHT

Ethan grinned, holding up his phone and pointing it at himself, giving his viewers a wave.

'Hi, everyone, and welcome to today's live-streaming vlog. I've got a very special guest with me today –' he turned the camera to point at me – 'would you look who it is, it's Flick Royale.'

I laughed, waving at the camera. 'Hey, Ethan.'

Be cool. Be cool. Be cool.

'So, we're standing in the beautiful Hotel Royale –' he spun the camera round to take in the lobby, watched closely by Matthew who was standing behind reception – 'and you live here, right?'

Be cool. Be cool. Be cool.

'That's right.' I smiled. 'I was just going out with my kind and gentle dog, Fritz. Want to come?'

'Sure.'

As I walked forwards, Fritz decided to trot around my ankles, tangling me in his lead and making me trip, lurching towards the door.

NOT COOL. NOT COOL. NOT COOL.

'Whoops!' I said, laughing nervously. 'Clumsy moment, we all have those, right? Ha ha ha!'

'Careful!' Ethan said with a smile, following me out of the door. 'So, Flick, tell us something about yourself that people might not know.'

'Hmmm that's a tricky one,' I replied, pretending I hadn't thought he'd ask me that. 'People might not know that I spend a lot of my free time helping out around the hotel!'

'That's cool,' he said, nodding, as I led him down the road to the crossing, ignoring those stopping to look at what we were doing. 'So, you grew up lending a hand behind the scenes? You must have been a great help to all the Hotel Royale staff.'

I thought about the time Cal and I hid the wooden spoons.

And the time I poured salt into all the sugar shakers.

And the time I let that peacock loose in the ballroom.

'Uh, well, I couldn't say,' I replied, swallowing the lump in my throat, before hurriedly adding. 'But I mostly learned last year, following the teams around the hotel because I was grounded—'

DANG IT. WHY DID I JUST SAY I WAS GROUNDED? The reason I was grounded was because

I broke into Prince Gustav's room, something I am TRYING to make the audience forget!

OK, play it cool, just casually steer the conversation in a different direction.

'Ah! Here we are! The road crossing!'

Ethan gave me a strange look.

QUICK. SAVE THE SITUATION.

A lady with grey hair in front of me began to step out into the road as the green man flashed and I took the perfectly presented opportunity to be a good person.

'Excuse me,' I said, cheerily, rushing up to offer her my arm. 'Can I help you cross the road?'

She looked up at me, stunned at first and then her expression transitioned to anger.

'How DARE you?' she cried, swatting me away. 'I'm only fifty-eight!'

'I'm so sorry!' I whimpered, blushing furiously as she hurried away from me across the road, muttering under her breath about rude teenagers. 'I didn't mean to . . . I . . .'

I turned to face the camera as Ethan stood frozen to the spot, clearly not knowing what to do. Others crossing the road, who had witnessed my humiliation, sniggered or shot me dirty looks as they passed, shaking their heads.

'Oh dear! Well, I think it's always better to risk insulting someone rather than be too afraid to offer your help! Right?' I croaked, attempting to sound chipper.

Ethan nodded in encouragement, saying, 'Right! I agree. So, you were saying you help out a lot around the hotel, which is fun. Bet you get some pretty cool guests.'

'Yeah, we do.' I nodded, dragging Fritz away from a biscuit wrapper he was trying to eat off the pavement. 'Yourself included.'

'Ah, you charmer,' he said, laughing and steadying the camera as we walked into the park. 'What's it like knowing that you're the heiress to Hotel Royale? Is it intimidating facing that kind of responsibility?'

I paused as I bent down to let Fritz off the lead. I hadn't thought of that question.

'Um, I suppose.'

Ethan gestured at me to keep talking, his eyes wide with interest.

'Other people grow up working out what they want to do whereas with me, I already know. And Hotel Royale is so famous and my mum is so good at running it that, you know, I don't want to muck it up. I guess I feel a bit pressured to be worthy of it and stuff.'

I hesitated, realising that I'd just gone on about something REALLY boring.

QUICK. Liven it up before everyone watching falls asleep!

'Anyway, enough of that yawn stuff.' I laughed, dropping my backpack off my shoulders and placing it down to unzip it. 'Another thing people might not know about me is how much I love animals. Obviously kind, gentle, non-vicious, well-trained Fritz is the love of my life . . .' Ethan followed my gaze with his camera, pointing it at Fritz who just happened at that moment to be doing a poop by a tree. 'Ah, um, ha, bad timing! I'll go and pick that up in a second because that's a very important responsibility of a dog owner.' I hesitated. 'Although obviously I won't do that on camera, because I'm sure your audience don't want to see that! Gross! Ha ha!'

OH MY GOD, WHAT ARE YOU SAYING, YOU CRAZY PERSON.

'As well as loving Fritz and all dogs,' I continued hurriedly, attempting to salvage the situation. 'I love birds! And during the winter months, for example January, like we're in now, it's important to make sure the birds are fed!'

Now, in my head, I imagined this to be a very picturesque scene.

I had asked Peter to stop off at the pet store on the way home from school, so I could buy a bag of bird seed in preparation for this very moment. I'd come up with it in the car and thought it would be a brilliant idea to show people that the 'real me' isn't someone who spends her life arguing over designer handbags, but in fact is someone who gives up her time to look after animals in need. I do love animals, so what better way to show that than feeding some birds in the park while Fritz frolics happily in the grass?

It would be just like that bit in *Mary Poppins*, when the kind old lady is feeding the birds and singing that nice, serene song. That was the vibe I was going for: calm, elegant, admirable.

That was not the vibe I got.

In fact, I think it's safe to say I achieved the exact opposite.

I scooped up a large handful of bird seed and gleefully threw it high, grinning broadly as it sprinkled down around me, scattering across the grass. I waited for the lovely birds to flock and peck happily at the food I had selflessly bought for them.

That did not happen.

Suddenly, all these pigeons came out of NOWHERE, and I mean there were HUNDREDS of them. They swooped down in a loud, squawking mass. I screamed and covered my head as they swarmed towards me from every angle, coming at me with their madly flapping wings. I hopped from one foot to the other and waved my arms around trying to get them to leave us alone, while

Ethan yelped and stumbled backwards, tripping over his feet and falling on to the grass, still filming the whole time.

Then, to make matters worse, a park warden came barrelling towards us, yelling, 'DON'T FEED THE BIRDS! DON'T FEED THE BIRDS! WHAT DO YOU THINK YOU'RE DOING?' and vigorously pointing at all the signs around the park that I hadn't ever noticed before and which said in big block capital letters: PLEASE DON'T FEED THE BIRDS.

Spotting the madness and not wanting to be left out, Fritz then bounded over to join in the fun, barking and chasing the pigeons around.

'No, Fritz!' I shouted, horrified, as he ran around in circles, snapping playfully as they flew away from him. 'Bad Fritz! Bad Fritz!'

As I began to chase Fritz in an attempt to catch him, still waving my arms around to bat away the pigeons trying to get at the feed scattered all over me, I saw Ethan, still lying on the ground, turn the camera to aim at his face.

'I'm afraid that's all we have time for!' he said, waving at the camera. 'From me and Flick, it's goodnight!'

And then he switched off his phone camera, lay his head back on the grass and closed his eyes.

'Well, if that doesn't catch everyone's attention,

Flick,' I heard Ethan say as Fritz hurtled past him, closely followed by myself and then the park warden, 'nothing ever will.'

NINE

TEENAGE HEIRESS IN BIZARRE BIRD FRENZY STUNT!

By Nancy Rose

She's already caused a stir with the now infamous HANDBAG-GATE scandal, and Felicity Royale has shocked once again with her bizarre bird-feeding escapades!

Last night, appearing on popular YouTuber Ethan Duke's live-streamed vlog, the heiress to Hotel Royale made the strange decision to PUBLICLY BREAK THE LAW by feeding the birds in a London park, flaunting her PURPOSEFUL REBELLION by standing in front of the DO NOT FEED THE BIRDS signs.

However, her RECKLESS BEHAVIOUR appeared to backfire as she soon became overwhelmed by the swarm of birds flocking towards her. Her FEROCIOUS sausage dog, Fritz, then appeared on the scene, attempting to MERCILESSLY EAT THE LONDON BIRDS straight out of the air.

At an earlier stage in the vlog – which has now gone globally viral and already sparked several spin-offs and memes across all social media platforms – the heiress also insulted an innocent pedestrian by commenting on her age.

This information may come as no surprise to those familiar with the aforementioned HANDBAG-GATE scandal, during which Miss Royale TACKLED this very reporter, Nancy Rose, to the ground in an attempt to STEAL a designer handbag, before her sausage dog launched a VICIOUS ATTACK.

Although Miss Royale is yet to comment on this recent incident, a source close to the teenager told me EXCLUSIVELY that this was not the first time Miss Royale has TROUBLED THE BIRD COMMUNITY: 'Once, she let a peacock loose in the hotel ballroom!'

For my full reaction, check out today's YouTube vlog at NancyRose and don't forget to subscribe for all the juiciest celeb gossip and their daily dramas!

★ ❀ ☽

'So,' Cal began, putting down his tray and sitting opposite me, 'what did you get up to last night, Flick? Quiet night in?'

I picked up a chip from my plate and threw it at him.

'I'm sorry, but you have to laugh.' He chuckled, dodging the chip as it flew past his ear.

'It is NOT FUNNY,' I seethed, knowing that my burning cheeks were likely to be as red as my hair. 'I wish people would stop *staring*.'

I glanced nervously at all the pairs of eyes blinking at me around the canteen.

'Don't they have anything else to talk about?' I grumbled.

'You'd think they would,' Olly said loudly, glaring at some sniggering students on the next table. 'And you'd think they'd know that staring is RUDE.'

They all quickly looked back at their food.

'Can I say something?' Cal asked, leaning forwards.

'No.'

'It's nice,' he said, breaking into a smile. 'I promise.'

'Fine,' I replied, rolling my eyes. Even though it was the last thing I felt like doing, I couldn't help but smile back.

It was his stupid dimples.

'I know the vlog didn't pan out as you thought it might, but I actually think it went really well.'

'Cal, I appreciate your optimism, but it was a total disaster! I'm the laughing stock of the entire country. I came across as the worst person in the world.' I grimaced. 'The RSPCA called the hotel this morning to let us know they're going to use the footage in their promo material as an excellent example of what not to do around animals.'

'I actually think you came across as very warm and funny,' Cal enthused.

'I agree.' Grace nodded next to me. 'Very . . . relatable.'

'It *was* supposed to show the real me,' I mumbled, pushing my food around the plate. 'Instead it just made it all worse.'

'It *was* the real you!' Cal emphasised. 'Come on, Flick – you make me laugh on a daily basis and last night you had the world in stitches.'

Grace shot him a warning look.

'I mean that nicely! Maybe I'm not saying it right.'

'No, I get what you mean,' Olly said, backing him up as Cal blushed. 'It was much better than some staged, perfectly scripted interview. Which is not you at all. It was completely . . . unexpected.'

'Have you spoken to Ethan today?' Grace asked cautiously.

'He's been messaging all day,' I replied, showing her my phone. 'He's been so lovely about the whole thing, but I feel terrible.'

'His message here says it's his most viewed vlog of all time!' Grace exclaimed, reading his recent text. 'He must be so excited! He couldn't ask for better publicity for his channel. That's great!'

She caught sight of my expression.

'Or . . . not so great,' she said, quickly passing my phone back to me.

'I guess that's good for Ethan.' I sighed. 'But it gets worse for me. Especially now Nancy Rose has found out about the peacock story.'

Cal laughed. I threw another chip at him.

'Hey!' he said as the chip hit him in the middle of his forehead. 'I love that story!'

'I'm not surprised, considering YOU were the one who dared me to let that peacock loose in the middle of a ball with members of parliament present!'

'That's not how I remember it,' he said, smiling mischievously. 'I'm sure it was your idea.'

'Either way, that's the second time someone "close" to me has given Nancy Rose a story about me,' I huffed. 'I think it might be Ella.'

'Ella?' Olly furrowed his brow. 'You really think she'd do something like that?'

'You *don't*? Only a handful of people know about the peacock incident AND the Prince Gustav incident. And she's the only one I can think of who'd want to feed information to Nancy Rose. Who else could it be? Anyway –' I sighed, feeling exhausted already even though it was only lunchtime – 'can we talk about something else?'

'No problem.' Cal nodded. 'This morning, we were actually discussing what story we can use for the front page of the first edition of the newspaper. You can help us.'

'But I don't have a role on the newspaper,' I reminded him.

'You don't have a role on the newspaper YET,' he replied sternly. 'And that doesn't matter. I'd want your opinion anyway.'

'All right,' I agreed. 'What are the options?'

'I suggested an exposé of the school kitchens,' Grace began.

'But –' Olly jumped in – 'they just got "outstanding" at the last inspection, so I don't think that would be interesting enough, especially not for the front page. I was thinking we could do a big debate piece on the music industry: for and against lip-syncing.'

Grace wrinkled her nose. 'That is completely irrelevant to the school.'

'I think it's interesting for the music pages, but I agree with Grace,' Cal said diplomatically. 'The front page has to get everyone in the school reaching for a copy. Something that piques their interest.'

'What about my idea?' an unwelcome voice squeaked.

I sighed as Ella's shadow fell over our table. I mean, really, my day could not get any worse.

'What idea?' Olly asked reluctantly, glancing at me.

'I texted Cal a suggestion for the front page last night,' she said brightly.

I felt a sharp pang at the idea of Cal and Ella texting. How did they even have each other's numbers? Before this week, she would never have admitted to knowing his name!

'So, did you like the idea?' she prompted, smiling at him.

Cal's ears turned pink at the attention as we all turned to face him.

'Sorry, Ella, it won't work.' He shifted in his chair.

Cal clearly thought her idea was terrible. It was very obvious that everyone wanted her to leave, but she didn't get it.

'I think it's really important that we include news that is actually *news*, you know? And as it's the first edition, we want to make sure it's something topical.'

I could barely look at her. Why was she lingering? Wasn't she at all *ashamed* that she'd been giving quotes to the press about one of her fellow students? What was WRONG with her?

'Yep,' Cal replied curtly, pushing food around his plate.

'It would be easy to ignore what's going on, so that we don't hurt anyone's feelings . . .'

I yawned loudly. Seriously, some people have no awareness.

'It's important to put personal relationships aside if we want this newspaper to be a success . . .'

They just have no idea when they're NOT WANTED.

'And we wouldn't be doing our jobs as journalists, if we ignored something this huge . . .'

They just can't pick up on a certain situation's vibes.

'Everyone would pick up a copy and the newspaper would be guaranteed to be a big success . . .'

It's a social skill that just can't be taught.

'So, if it's difficult for you, I'm happy to write the feature on Nancy Rose and Flick.

Wait. WHAT?

I snapped my head up so fast, I swear I heard something in my shoulder click, and if that has caused permanent muscle damage, I will be taking Ella to court.

'Sorry, what did you say?'

'The feature on you and Nancy,' she told me, her eyes all wide and innocent. 'Didn't Cal tell you it was in the pipeline?'

I turned to him. 'Is she serious?'

'No, like I said, I don't think it's for us,' Cal said hurriedly, his eyes full of worry.

'You don't *think* it's for you?' I practically yelled. 'Well, that's VERY comforting.'

'You know that's not what I meant.'

'I don't see why you're so upset, Flick,' Ella said, acting all shocked. 'Isn't making headlines and being the centre of attention exactly what you want? Some free publicity is surely right up your street.'

I was so gobsmacked; I couldn't think of a word to say.

'And don't worry,' Ella continued, smiling down at me. 'When I write the feature, I'll be sure to capture the *real* you.'

TEN

Sky, have you seen it?

The puma?

WHAT? How do YOU
know about the puma?
You don't even live
in this country!

I saw it on the news.
Apparently, it escaped
from a private owner

I'm not talking
about the puma

Who would own a puma?!
Just get a cat! Poor thing is
probably terrified in London

I'M NOT TALKING
ABOUT THE PUMA.
I'm talking about my vlog
with Ethan

Yeah, I've seen it . . .
it's hard to miss! I meant to text
you earlier to tell you how much
I loved it but I got distracted by
Gustav deciding to call for the
first time in forever . . . Anyway,
the vlog is great! Live-streaming
was a genius idea

Be serious please.
This isn't a joke

I am serious!!
It is HILARIOUS

No, it's a DISASTER.
How do I fix it??

Fix what?! I think it's brilliant! The pigeons, the park guard and then you chasing Fritz . . . it's like a scene out of a sitcom!!

It was supposed to prove that what everyone is saying is WRONG. Instead, it's just backed up my image as a horrible diva who doesn't deserve to be on an Heirs to Watch list!! I have to do something. Any ideas?

You know, if you found the lost puma, you would DEFINITELY get back on that list

WHY DOES EVERYONE KEEP TALKING ABOUT THE PUMA?! I have a serious problem at hand and everyone

Hang on. The doorbell just went

Who is it?

No idea, Mum's got it. Anyway, as I was saying, I have a serious

Oh my god

What?

I know that voice

What voice?

The voice at the door.
It can't be

Who? Who is it?

No way, it can't be her

WHO IS HER???

Is it really her?!

WHO??????

I actually think it is her!
I have to go!

NO! TELL ME WHO IT IS

WHOOOOO ISSSSSS ITTTTTTT??????

★ ❀ ☾

'Well, if it isn't my favourite niece.'

Aunt Hazel stood in the hall with her arms wide open as I poked my head out my bedroom door. Standing next to her, Mum looked as though someone had slapped her around the face.

'I can't believe you're here!' I said excitedly, rushing over so that she could give me two air kisses. 'Are you staying with us?'

'Of course!' She grinned. 'That lovely head concierge, Marvin, put me in the Sapphire Suite as normal.'

'Matthew,' Mum corrected through gritted teeth. 'And there's no way you're staying in the Sapphire Suite, Hazel. You're very welcome to stay at the hotel, but you're going to have to move to —'

'Honestly, Christine.' Hazel sighed, rolling her eyes and swanning past me to sit down on the sofa. 'I've been here all of five seconds and you're already nagging me. You get more and more like Mum every day.'

Mum pursed her lips so hard they disappeared, before she grumpily muttered, 'I do NOT nag like Mum.'

'So, Flick, come and sit down next to me.' Hazel smiled, patting the sofa beside her. 'It has been how many years? I know it sounds clichéd, but I can't believe how much you've grown!'

'It has been four years since you last dropped in,' Mum seethed. 'And about two years since you called.'

'You have no idea how busy I've been in New York,' Hazel said, leaning back into the cushions. 'And, if I'm not mistaken, phone calls work both ways, Christine.'

Mum slumped down into the chair opposite us and glared at Hazel. Mum had always said that, growing up, she had never got on with her younger sister and only sibling, who she labelled the 'wild child' of the family, and that it was better for everybody's sanity that they lived in different countries.

It meant that I hardly knew my aunt at all. I knew from the very few times that she'd come back to England and stayed at the hotel that she was incredibly glamorous and very demanding, with a knack for causing a LOT of scandal, but that was about it. Last time she stayed all those years ago, I thought she was so fabulous with her beautiful clothes and her carefree attitude, that I'd told Matthew I wanted to be just like her when I grew up.

He'd given me a look and said in this tired voice, 'Lord help us.'

Lounging on our sofa in her long cream high-neck coat and diamond earrings, her hair perfectly curled about her shoulders, she was just how I remembered.

'How long are you staying?' Mum asked, patting her lap for Fritz to jump up and give her a comforting cuddle.

'What a precious dog! I've always loved poodles.'

'He's a dachshund,' Mum corrected. 'And don't avoid my question.'

'What question?'

'How long are you staying? Two days? One day? A few hours? A couple of minutes?'

'Indefinitely.'

Mum started. '*Indefinitely*?'

'Yes. I'm here for as long as Flick needs me,' she said, her eyes twinkling at me.

'Flick?' Mum looked at me, baffled. 'What has FLICK got to do with anything?'

'Well, someone has to help her on this exciting new path and I could hardly leave her glittering career in *your* hands, now could I?' Hazel raised her eyebrows. 'I know you well enough, Christine, to know that you'd prefer to hide her away and wait for everything to blow over, rather than take a red-hot opportunity and turn it into whatever Flick wants it to be.'

'Hazel,' Mum began, sitting up and disturbing Fritz who had curled into a ball on her lap, 'what are you talking about?'

'What do you mean "glittering career"?' I asked.

'You see? This is exactly why you both need me,' she said, chuckling. 'Flick, your little scuffle with Nancy Rose was the perfect launch pad into the public eye and, at first, I admit I was concerned that you would just apologise and sweep it under the carpet, likely on instruction from your mother –' she shot Mum a pointed glance – 'and of course, being dropped from the "50 Heirs to Watch" list wasn't exactly ideal . . .'

'I was hoping to prove they'd got me all wrong through a guest spot on Ethan's vlog,' I admitted, embarrassed, 'but then —'

'But then the disastrous vlog came out and you've managed to maintain your spot in the limelight. Excellent work,' Hazel declared cheerily, patting my hand.

'But, like you said, that vlog was disastrous,' I pointed out, confused.

'A little rough around the edges, yes, but now I'm here, that's all going to change. You leave it with me, Flick, and soon enough we'll make the judges of that ridiculous heirs list rue the day they dropped a Royale from their ranks! If they think you're not one to watch, then they are seriously shortsighted.'

'Hazel . . .' Mum said, narrowing her eyes at her, but I cut in before she could continue.

'Are you saying that you have an idea to help me?' I asked hopefully, suddenly seeing a light at the end of my so-far catastrophic tunnel.

'Absolutely. I've got the perfect plan to show everyone *exactly* who you really are.' Hazel smiled, gripping my hand excitedly. 'Just you wait and see.'

ELEVEN

The next morning before school, Hazel accosted me as I walked across the lobby.

'Good morning, Flick,' she said cheerfully, clacking over in her emerald-green stilettos and looping her arm through mine. 'On your way to school?'

I nodded. 'How did you sleep?'

'Oh, never mind all that, you don't have anything planned for after school, do you?'

'No, why?'

She brought us to a halt as we reached the door. 'Because I have set up a VERY exciting meeting for you, so as soon as school ends, come straight back home and don't be late.'

'What meeting?' I asked eagerly.

'You'll see,' she said, clapping her hands. 'And this is just the beginning. Have a good day, darling!'

When I got to school, I found Grace and filled her in straight away.

'That is so cool!' she said with a gasp, after I told her

about the mysterious meeting. 'Who do you think it's with?'

'I don't know,' I said, biting my lip. 'Maybe with the producers of *Morning Sunshine*? You know, to tell them my side of the story. Maybe she's managed to persuade them that Nancy Rose's portrayal of me is completely off!'

'Maybe it's a big endorsement deal!' Grace suggested. 'For bird food or something!'

I winced, remembering all those flapping wings. 'Eugh, I hope not.'

'OR,' said Grace, her eyes widening in excitement, 'you could be heading into the jungle! You are totally a celebrity now! IMAGINE!'

'You really think I'm famous enough for the jungle?'

'Yes! That vlog of you being attacked by pigeons is EVERYWHERE. If the meeting does turn out to be about the jungle, you have to tell me immediately so we can prepare you for it. You can come over and I can let Bruce sit on your head for a few minutes or something.'

'I'm not sure that putting your docile tortoise on my head for a few minutes would prepare me for weeks in a jungle with all those creepy crawlies.' I shivered. 'Gross.'

'I can't believe you're going to the jungle!' Grace squealed, jumping up and down on the spot.

'Grace,' I shushed her, glancing around to check no one in the corridor was listening, 'we don't know that's what the meeting is about yet. It could be nothing to do with going to the jungle.'

'You're right,' she said, closing her eyes and fanning herself. 'We shouldn't get carried away.' She hesitated and then grabbed my wrists again. 'OMG, what's your ballroom dancing like?'

'What's this about dancing?' Olly asked, coming over with Cal. 'I'm the one in the family who's got the moves, right, Grace?'

Grace scowled and turned to me. 'Remind me again why we always have to hang out with my brother?'

'Because I'm devastatingly handsome?'

'Don't forget your modesty and humble nature,' Cal pointed out, winking at Grace.

'But of course.' Olly grinned. 'What can I say? I'm irresistible.'

I laughed along with Olly, but was sure not to make any eye contact with Cal.

I was still grumpy with him for not shooting Ella down completely about her ridiculous front-page feature idea, and no matter how many times he told me that he wasn't entertaining it, I still felt annoyed, especially when she'd made it so clear that she was the one giving quotes to Nancy Rose. HELLO, why else would she have made that pointed comment about her feature capturing the

109

'real me'? That's EXACTLY what Nancy Rose's source had said! She had practically admitted her guilt right there in front of everyone and Cal STILL wasn't convinced it was her.

Every time I thought about Ella wrapping Cal around her little finger, my stomach felt like it was being sharply twisted.

'Tell them your exciting news,' Cal prompted Olly, nudging him with his elbow.

'It's not that exciting,' Olly said quickly, catching my eye and blushing.

'Ah, you see? Modest after all.' Cal laughed. 'Olly's band has been booked for a gig. Isn't that cool?'

'Are you serious?' Grace said. 'That's amazing!'

'It's just a gig for emerging bands.' He shrugged. 'Nothing massive. But should be a lot of fun.'

'He's playing it down. The bands are selected and it's hugely competitive. One of the organisers came across the song Olly put up on YouTube and invited them to perform,' Cal enthused. 'It's in a few weeks.'

'Wow, Olly!' I smiled. 'That's brilliant, well done! We'll all be there, cheering you on.'

He beamed back at me.

'Flick has some exciting news too,' Grace informed them. 'She's got a big, important meeting after school today that her aunt Hazel has set up.'

'What kind of meeting?'

'I couldn't say.' I sniffed.

A knowing grin spread across Cal's face. 'You don't know what the meeting is about, do you?'

'Of course I know what the meeting is!' I blurted.

I'm not sure why I lied. Again, I blame the dimples. They're very distracting. And annoying.

'I just wouldn't want to tell someone who might splash it all over the front page of a newspaper,' I added pointedly.

'Come on, Flick.' He sighed impatiently. 'You know I would never do that.'

'Oh yes, that's right. You'd just get your new friend, *Ella*, to do it instead. Why don't you text her now to let her know? I know you like to stay in touch.'

'My number was on the email I sent out to these guys with all the notes from our first brainstorm meeting,' he said. 'She just took it off there.'

'I don't remember receiving any newspaper email,' I said, folding my arms.

'Because I didn't think you'd want to!' he argued, looking exasperated. 'You did nothing in that first meeting except glare at Ella and then tell me off afterwards for letting her on to the team. I'm pretty sure you even said you didn't want a role on the newspaper, if Ella was involved. So I assumed —'

'I said that because I have PRINCIPLES!'

'Look, if you want to have a role on the newspaper, then obviously I would love for you to —'

'I DON'T want a role on your newspaper.'

'Fine!'

'FINE!'

'Flick—' Olly began as Cal rolled his eyes.

'I'd love to stay and chat, but I have to go and prepare for my very important meeting. Which is about important things. And with important people. Bye.'

And then I marched away for effect, without having any clue where I was going, so I ended up just going to my lesson ten minutes early and sitting there being annoyed.

But that didn't matter, it was all about the principle and I had totally won. I managed to avoid Cal for the rest of the day and, as soon as the last bell rang to signal the end of school, I rushed out of the building, climbed into the car and told Peter we would NOT be waiting for him.

Firstly, because I didn't want to be late for my important meeting and, secondly, because Cal's a big pig-head.

Hazel was waiting for me in the lobby as I arrived home, with Audrey watching her from behind reception like a hawk. Audrey is not a big fan of Hazel. On Hazel's last visit, she'd booked a load of salsa dancers to entertain her dinner guests without telling anyone and, when Audrey went in to the dining room to tell them to stop, she was accidentally hit in the face with a maraca.

She's never quite forgiven Hazel for that one.

'There you are!' Hazel exclaimed as Matthew guided me through the door, still having to shield me from the few reporters hanging determinedly around the hotel.

'Is Cal at a newspaper meeting?' Matthew asked, looking confused at his son's absence.

'Cal is making his own way back from school this evening,' I told him.

'Ah.' He chuckled knowingly. 'What did he do this time?'

'I just feel that he really doesn't —'

'Sorry, Flick, I hate to rush you,' Hazel cut in, pulling me away from Matthew, 'but they're waiting for us in the dining room. Come along.'

'Who are waiting?' I asked, but she ignored me, swanning ahead.

I followed nervously, brushing any stray Fritz hairs off my school jumper and running a hand through my hair, even though I'd brushed it a hundred times in the car.

Mum was sitting at one of the dining tables opposite a man and a woman I'd never seen before. They stood up straight away when Hazel and I walked in, and the woman immediately held out her hand to take mine.

'Flick, what a pleasure to meet you,' she said, shaking my hand VERY enthusiastically. 'I'm Tanya, and this is my assistant, Michael.'

I shook Michael's hand too and then sat down in between Mum and Hazel.

'Flick, Tanya and Michael are television producers.' Hazel smiled, as Timothy went around the table filling up everyone's glasses with water.

'Wow! Cool!' I blurted out.

I mean, I couldn't have sounded more like a loser and I noticed Hazel wince at my reaction. They didn't really look like television producers, at least not how I always thought television producers would look. You know, the kind of people who dress in smart tailored jackets, not a hair out of place, and have Bluetooth headsets attached to their ears so they're never actually off the phone. But they weren't like that at all. Michael was wearing a very casual T-shirt, jeans and a beanie, and Tanya was wearing bright clashing colours and had a super-cool nose ring.

Teachers were totally lying to us when they said piercings weren't suitable for interviews.

'It's nice to meet you,' I said quickly in my most grown-up voice, hoping to make up for the *wow, cool* thing.

Mum was watching them with the same expression

she wears whenever we play Monopoly at Christmas: interested, with a hint of mistrust. 'It's all about value gained for price paid,' she says every year when she gets out the box. 'Pay attention to cost, not just cash flow.'

Seriously, if you want to suck all of the fun out of Monopoly, play it with a real-life hotel owner.

'What is this all about?' Mum said sternly, receiving a sharp look from her sister.

'Really, Christine, we haven't even ordered our starters yet and you're already talking business.' Hazel chuckled. 'May I recommend the goats' cheese, it's to die for.'

'We're happy to get straight down to it,' Tanya said, as Michael nodded in agreement. 'Flick, we would like to talk to you about doing a pilot for your own reality TV show.'

My jaw dropped. 'W . . . what?'

'That vlog with Ethan Duke?' Michael grinned. 'Television gold.'

'Your story has captured our imaginations. The heiress to all this,' Tanya said, gesturing around us. 'We'd like to pitch a reality show all about you to some networks. Following your glamorous lifestyle. It would be like the British Kardashians, but with fewer family members.'

WHAT? MY OWN SHOW?

Oh my God.

I sat in complete shock, staring at Tanya who was nodding encouragingly at me.

'You want to follow my daughter with a bunch of cameras?' Mum asked, looking as baffled as I felt.

'Yes, we do, Ms Royale.' Tanya nodded, turning to her. 'We feel there is huge potential in Flick to be a reality TV star.'

'You . . . you do?' I squeaked, my heart thudding against my chest.

'Of course, the show might not get picked up,' Tanya said matter-of-factly. 'We'd start by filming a pilot and working out the structure of the show. If that was successful, then we'd be looking at an entire series.'

AN ENTIRE SERIES. ABOUT ME.

'And if that did well,' Hazel said, her eyes glittering at me, 'you'd get everything else that comes along with being a reality TV star. A perfume range, clothes line, book deal and who knows what else?'

I was freaking out. And I mean, FREAKING OUT. My own TV show? Seriously? A show about ME? This was a dream come true. This was PERFECT.

Because what better way to show everyone that I am not the selfish, undeserving heiress that they think I am than with my OWN TV SHOW? It was exactly the platform I needed to prove to everyone that they were wrong about me being a diva and a Handbag Hooligan!

Plus, a perfume range would be AWESOME.

'Absolutely not,' Mum said, interrupting my excited thought process. 'Thank you for your time, but I don't think so.'

'Mum! Please!' I begged, as Tanya and Michael shared a glance. 'My own TV show!'

'You can't seriously be considering this, Flick.' Mum looked stunned. 'After handbag-gate and the social-media trolls!'

'This is the perfect opportunity to turn it into positive attention!'

Mum looked unconvinced.

'Christine,' Hazel said calmly, perusing the menu. 'I think you owe it to Flick to at least consider it. After all, it is her, not you, at the centre of all this, so I'd suggest she deserves to have a say in her future. Wouldn't you?'

As Mum stared at her sister across the table, I truly understood the meaning of that phrase, 'if looks could kill'.

But something Hazel said must have got through to her because she inhaled deeply and growled, 'Fine, we'll discuss it.'

'Marvellous!' Hazel smiled while Tanya and Michael both picked up their menus, satisfied. 'Now, let's get that charming young waiter to take us through the specials.'

As she caught Timothy's attention and he came hurrying over, she winked at me across the table. I was so happy, I felt like I was glowing.

Everything was finally looking UP.

TWELVE

I wish I had never gone to Cal's stupid newspaper meeting.

I was having a brilliant day, daydreaming all about the meeting the night before and what my very own TV show would be like, and then Ella had to go ahead and ruin everything, as usual.

Mum had made me promise not to tell anyone about the TV show quite yet as it was still in the very early stages, blah blah blah. I was only allowed to tell Grace, partly because I was too excited not to tell anyone and partly because Grace had sent me loads of texts asking whether or not I was going to the jungle.

Grace was so overwhelmed when I phoned her, she screamed everything she said for the entire conversation.

She promised not to tell anyone but the whole of the next day at school, every time she saw me, her eyes bulged right out of her head and she kept letting out these little squeaks, as though she might explode from the secret.

I wasn't planning on going to the newspaper meeting after school, because I had said to Cal literally the day

119

before that I had no interest in having a role on his team and everything, but THEN Grace happened to mention that their agenda for the meeting was to discuss layout and also some new ideas that Ella had come forward with.

There was no WAY I wasn't going to go when I heard that.

I could picture her headline suggestions:

FLICK ROYALE vs MARIAH: WHO IS THE BIGGEST DIVA OF THEM ALL?

SECRETS, SHAME AND SCANDAL: THE REAL FLICK ROYALE

WHEN TRUE COLOURS SHOW: WHAT REALLY HAPPENED THE NIGHT OF HANDBAG-GATE

'HOTEL ROYALE HEIRESS LEFT ME FIGHTING FOR MY LIFE!' EXCLUSIVE INTERVIEW WITH NANCY ROSE

So obviously I had to go along to make sure she didn't think about pitching anything along those lines, and that if she did, I was there to shout 'SLANDER' at all the right moments.

If there had still been any doubt that Ella was using Cal's newspaper to turn my friends against me along with the rest of the nation, then that was completely wiped out the minute I walked into the meeting because you know what she was doing?

Standing with Cal at the front of the room, laughing. LAUGHING. As though Cal had said something FUNNY. And do you know what happened then? She said something and HE started laughing.

Cal! Ella! Laughing! Together!

I must have gone pale, because Grace stopped yabbering on about whatever she was talking about when we were walking in to ask me if I was all right.

'I'm FINE,' I said loudly, hoping Cal would hear.

But he couldn't possibly over the exaggerated laughter coming from Ella, twisting the knife even further into my stomach. There was no chance she found anything Cal said *that* funny, she thought he was the biggest loser in school. It was so obvious she was just trying to wind me up.

Well, her plan was failing because she wasn't getting to me AT ALL.

And, not that I care, but when you laugh with

someone, you do NOT need to casually touch the other person's arm like she was doing. That's an invasion of personal space and if she did that more than once, Cal could SUE.

Also, I've never heard her laugh like that before. She was definitely putting on that laugh. Why was it so high and squeaky like a giggly hamster? Ugh, that laugh was the worst laugh EVER. I am so grateful I do not sound like a hamster when I laugh. Who wants to sound like a hamster? How could Cal stand there listening to that hamster laugh?

'Are you sure you're OK, Flick?' Grace asked as I sat down next to her and Olly.

'I don't even LIKE hamsters.'

Grace blinked at me. 'Huh?'

'Never mind,' I grumbled, tapping my nails impatiently on the table.

'Are you getting a hamster?' Grace asked excitedly.

Olly looked up from his notes. 'What's this about hamsters?'

'Flick is getting a hamster.'

'Fritz won't like that,' Olly pointed out. 'He hates squirrels, and hamsters are like a mini version of squirrels without the big tail. Why don't you get something cool like a lizard?'

'Ooooh.' Grace nodded. 'Maybe an iguana!'

'Flick's getting an iguana?' Cal asked, FINALLY deciding to end the rollicking conversation he'd been having with laugh-a-minute Ella. 'Seriously? An iguana?'

'And?' I huffed, narrowing my eyes at him. 'You think I can't handle one because I'm just this selfish diva who cares about no one else, not even iguanas?'

Cal held up his hands. 'Whoa, I was just —'

'You know what, Cal? You are wrong about me. And I can handle an iguana.'

'OK, then.' He laughed, looking at me strangely. 'Anyway, I'm pleased you're here, Flick. Shall we start the meeting?'

Ella decided to go and sit on the other side of the classroom from me, which I was very grateful for because, should Cal say anything witty, I wouldn't want that hamster laugh piercing my ear drums.

Cal started off the meeting with his plans for the layouts, but I was too distracted by Ella to listen to what he was saying.

She was leaning forwards on her desk, with her chin cupped in her hand, nodding along. I glanced from her to Cal and back to her again, trying to work out if he was looking at her more than anyone else. I felt confident that he wouldn't be taken in by those fake, innocent doe eyes she was putting on. He was much too smart. He knew what Ella was really like; he always said she was a typical Queen Bee who liked to put people down to make herself look better. *He* had told *me* that only last term.

He wouldn't just forget all those times she'd been mean to him and actually start to *like* her.

Would he?

'Ella, I thought your idea for the best ways to accessorise the school uniform without getting in trouble was brilliant,' Cal said, nodding at her. 'Were you thinking illustrations or photo images?'

'I thought photos would be more striking,' she announced, addressing everyone in the room. 'I am very happy to model each look.'

She caught me rolling my eyes and for a moment her expression soured before she swivelled in her chair to face Cal and asked, 'On another note, have you considered my suggestion for the front-page story?'

Cal opened his mouth to speak but I saved him the trouble.

'Of course he hasn't considered it,' I fumed, my cheeks growing hot.

'Well, then, he's not the journalist I thought he was,' she retaliated.

'I—'

'And what kind of journalist is that?' I demanded, cutting Cal off before he could say anything. 'The kind that embellishes stories to get more clicks? The kind that listens to "sources" who have no idea what they're talking about and have their own evil agenda?'

Ella narrowed her eyes at me. 'What are you even talking about? Journalists are supposed to report on the news. Things that are relevant! It's not our fault that you keep publicly humiliating yourself!'

'Can —'

'Well, you know what, Ella?' I seethed, interrupting Cal again. 'I am relevant because I'm about to be the star of my very own reality TV show.'

Olly's jaw dropped. Ella physically recoiled. Cal stared at me. And Grace jumped to her feet and punched the air, squealing at the top of her lungs.

'Yaaaaaaaaaaaaaaaaaaaaas!' she cried, breaking into a little dance. 'WE CAN TALK ABOUT IT! I've been holding it in ALL DAY!'

'A TV show?' Olly asked, his eyes wide with awe. 'Really?'

'That's right,' I said, crossing my arms triumphantly. 'So, instead of writing a feature about handbag-gate or OLD news like that, why don't you ask me to do an interview all about my exciting new reality TV show?'

Grace's arm shot up in the air. 'Me! Let me interview you! Me! Pick me!'

'All right, Grace.' I nodded, before turning to look pointedly at Cal and saying, 'I'll *consider* it, depending on whether I *think* it's for me.'

I picked up my bag from under my chair and walked towards the classroom door.

'Wait, Flick,' Cal said hurriedly, as I reached the door. 'Where are you going?'

I stopped, took a deep breath, turned round and declared, 'I QUIT!' all dramatically.

Even though, *technically*, I didn't have a role to quit.

But that's not important.

After revelling in their stunned expressions, I turned on my heel and swanned right out of there, my jacket slung over my shoulder and everything.

Which, quite frankly, is further proof that I really do deserve my own show.

My talents are wasted on these people.

THIRTEEN

Persuading Mum to let me film the TV pilot proved to be VERY difficult.

Which was especially awkward now that I'd told my friends all about it. Once I'd calmed down a bit from the whole 'I QUIT' scenario, I had to text Grace and get her to swear them all to secrecy as nothing had been signed yet.

Even though Grace said she made Ella promise, I didn't have much hope, but there was nothing I could do about that and, if anything, Ella knowing about the TV show made me even more determined to get Mum on board.

Ella would never let me live it down otherwise. You can imagine the headline she would pitch:

IT'S A NO SHOW!
FLICK ROYALE'S "REALITY SHOW" FAILS TO
MATERIALISE! EVER!

I could NOT give her that satisfaction.

Every evening, I'd remind Mum that Tanya and Michael were still waiting for confirmation that we could go ahead with a pilot and she'd let out a long sigh, look me right in the eye and ask, 'Is it really what you want, though, Flick?'

And every night, I'd reply, 'ARE YOU INSANE? Of course this is what I want! How else am I going to prove to everyone that I'm not a Handbag Hooligan and I don't go around disturbing the bird community on a daily basis?'

But she kept saying that I hadn't thought it all through and that the TV-show process probably wouldn't be as smooth as I imagined it would.

'Why do you keep saying that?' I asked her one night, when she'd repeated it twice that day. 'Do you have production experience or something?'

'No, it's just this has all come from Hazel and trust me, when it comes to my sister, nothing is ever as simple as it seems,' she said, knowingly. 'She has a knack of viewing everything through rose-tinted glasses and then making a run for it at the first sign of any complication.'

'OK, firstly, you know how sensitive I am to the word "rose" right now because of Nancy, so quite frankly, you should be a bit more careful in future, and secondly, maybe you should give Hazel a little more credit,' I said in exasperation. 'Don't you think you're being a bit hard on her?'

'Flick, I know you're convinced that this TV show is

the answer to your problems but I'm worried that it's just going to magnify them.'

'Magnify?' I put my hands on my hips. 'What do you mean?'

'You keep saying having your own show will prove everyone wrong but what if . . .' She trailed off.

'What if it proves everyone right? Is that what you're saying? That I'll come across badly?'

'No, Flick, not on purpose. But you hear things about the way reality television is edited and I'm scared it won't portray you as honestly as you're hoping and then you'll get hurt.' She bit her lip. 'I'll tell you what. I'm not saying no, but before we make a decision, why don't you write out a list of all the advantages and disadvantages of filming this pilot.'

'OK.' I nodded. 'That seems fair.'

'And you have to be *honest*,' she emphasised. 'Think it through properly and then we'll have another chat about it, OK?'

So, I did what she said and the next day I left the following on her desk:

Reasons we should say YES to Flick's TV show

1.   Flick's reputation is currently in the GUTTER because of handbag-gate, illegally feeding birds and insulting strangers. This will make it all better and people will like her again!

2.   Ditto for Fritz.

3.   The show will put a stop to MEAN people at school being MEAN about Flick in school newspapers and will stop these MEAN people from turning Flick's friends against her. (I won't name names because I'm classy. But Ella has really crossed the line this time.)

4.   The show will provide FUTURE CAREER OPPORTUNITIES such as (but not limited to) perfume and fashion lines, lucrative book deals, going into jungles and eating bugs.

5.   It is EXCELLENT PUBLICITY for the beautiful setting of Hotel Royale – people will see the show and then flock from far and wide to stay here, so it is GOOD FOR BUSINESS.

Reasons we should say NO to Flick's TV show

1. It MIGHT be edited badly and MIGHT make Flick's reputation worse.
2. Ditto for Fritz.

Mum came into my bedroom the evening after I'd left the note, when I was very busy working out if I could pull off a beret.

'Don't you look adorable.' She smiled, brushing past me as I stood in front of the mirror and slumping down on my bed. Fritz jumped up from his basket to greet her.

'Wow!' I exclaimed, taking in her outfit. She was wearing a long blue gown and had her hair done up prettily, showing off her sparkling diamond earrings.

'You think?' She brushed down the skirt of her dress and was careful not to let Fritz jump up on her. After several attempts, he grumpily went back to his basket to sulk. 'We're hosting a black-tie dinner downstairs. Nice hat.'

'Adorable wasn't exactly the vibe I was going for,' I admitted, turning back to my reflection and pushing the beret over to the side of my head slightly. 'Maybe if I wear it on a tilt? Hmm, maybe not. I look like I'm joining the cadets.'

'I got your list,' she said, as I tossed the beret on to the floor.

Fritz immediately went to inspect the beret and, on deciding it wasn't edible, he curled tightly inside it and turned it into his new bed. He is so creative sometimes.

'What do you think?' I asked, going to sit down next to Mum, careful not to crease her dress.

'I think that clearly you really want to film this pilot,' she said, sighing.

'I *really* do.'

'So, I've come to the following decision.' She took a deep breath. 'I will give my permission for one pilot episode to be filmed as a trial. Just one episode, Flick. No more. And only if it doesn't get in the way of school. Once we see how that turns out and whether or not it's working well for you in general, we'll go from there regarding the rest of the series.'

I inhaled sharply. 'You mean it? I can do the show?'

'You can do the pilot,' she amended. 'On a trial basis.'

'AHHHHHHHHHHHHHH!' I gleefully lunged forwards at her, knocking her backwards on the bed and causing Fritz to suddenly get very excited. He scrambled out of the beret to join us, barking and leaping up on to the bed, sticking his little wet nose right into Mum's ear.

'Ooof! Fritz, no!' she cried, pushing him towards me.

'Thanks so much, Mum!' I laughed, cuddling Fritz to my chest and letting him lick my face happily. 'This is the best news EVER. I'll call Tanya now! Is Hazel in? I'll go and tell her too.'

'I believe she's out with an ambassador at the theatre this evening,' Mum said in a strained voice. 'She instructed Matthew to get the tickets this morning, even though she knew it was sold out. Lucky for her, Matthew has his ways. Right, I had better get downstairs before the guests arrive.'

'Thanks so much, Mum.' I gave her another hug as she stood up. 'You won't regret this.'

'I hope not,' she said, kissing my hair. 'By the way, before I forget, I bumped into Cal the other day.'

'Oh?' I scrolled through my contacts for Tanya's number.

'He seemed worried. He was looking for you. He said he'd tried calling?'

I shrugged. 'I must have been busy. I'm sure it was nothing. Anyway, have a good night!'

'I couldn't help but notice that point on your list about your friends turning against you because of all the handbag-gate, diva nonsense,' she said, raising her eyebrows. 'I just thought I'd check you weren't talking about Cal.'

'You're going to be late.'

'I know you've had your differences in the past, but you grew up together. You can't possibly believe that Cal might think badly of you, because of all that silliness?'

'Tanya, hi!' I said, as she picked up. 'I've got some amazing news!'

Mum nodded and shrugged, shutting my bedroom door behind her. As Tanya cheered down the phone and took me through the next steps, I felt relieved that I hadn't had to answer Mum's question about Cal and what he thought of me.

Because the truth was, right now, I really wasn't sure what that answer would be.

FOURTEEN

The next day, I made my way down via the lobby to snaffle some breakfast, fully expecting the lift doors to open to the usual serene atmosphere of Saturday morning reception: the classical piano tinkling prettily in the background; porters nodding hello as they trundled past with their golden trolleys piled with luggage; Matthew on the phone behind the front desk, polishing the surface as he noted down another booking; and smartly dressed guests on their way to the dining room, quietly marvelling at all the freshly arranged flowers that had gracefully appeared in the lobby overnight.

That's not what happened.

Instead, as the lift doors slid open, I stepped out into a whirlwind of noise and disorder.

There were all these men and women dressed in black T-shirts, speaking loudly into headsets and bossing each other around, as guests dodged around them curiously. A cluster of them stood by reception, holding a load of camera and sound equipment, and speaking to Audrey,

135

who looked tense and uncomfortable, while Matthew politely begged them not to put their cameras on the reception surface as they were leaving marks.

'What the . . .' I gasped, frozen to the spot as I took it all in.

'Flick! There you are!' Tanya waved at me, bustling over with Michael and gesturing to a tall, thin woman with a sharp bob haircut, wearing a tailored trouser suit. 'This is Francine, she's the director of your pilot. Francine, this is Flick.'

'Good to meet you,' Francine said busily, before telling one of the crew members to fetch her bag.

'What's going on?' I asked, shaking Francine's hand.

'You're doing a TV show, remember?' Tanya laughed. 'We're setting up and doing some scouting. Francine needs to get her bearings of the hotel so we know where to film each scene.'

'Who are all these people? Does Mum know you're here?'

'Don't worry, Hazel is around somewhere. There she is!' Michael waved at my aunt, who was busy telling some of the crew members all about the chandeliers and advising them on where to get the best angle of the reception area.

'Flick, you're up!' she said, swanning over and kissing

me on the cheek. 'Don't worry, Francine, we'll be sorting out her wardrobe before we start filming. Tanya, you were going to recommend a make-up artist, weren't you? We need to really make her eyes pop. Now, when did you want to discuss content? Flick and I have plenty of ideas.'

'I —'

'Where is what's-his-name?' Hazel asked impatiently, cutting across me. 'You know, the butler, Thomas or something.'

'Timothy? He's not a butler, he's —'

'There he is! Francine, this is Thomas. He's Flick's butler.'

Timothy looked as baffled as I felt as he dutifully came over to meet Francine.

'Timothy isn't my butler,' I corrected. 'He's actually one of the best —'

'Flick.' Audrey came clacking over. 'We need to —'

'We don't have time for any minor details.' Hazel sighed. 'Which conference room is free for Francine and me to discuss the ins and outs?'

'You didn't book a conference room this morning,' Audrey informed her calmly, glancing at me. 'They're all booked, I'm afraid. Perhaps we can accommodate you elsewhere, and I would be grateful if the crew could move out of reception, as they are disturbing our guests. We were assured that that wouldn't be the case.'

'Of course,' Tanya said hurriedly, giving a sharp nod to Michael who immediately rushed off, speaking into his headset.

'We need to do some stock shots of the hotel,' Francine said. 'They won't take long.'

'Well, perhaps you could do those at a more appropriate time, say, in the early hours of the morning, when there will be fewer guests wandering around, disturbing your shots. I'm very happy for you to call me and schedule that in,' Audrey said firmly. 'Tanya, shall I help you and Michael escort the crew out of the hotel?'

One of Audrey's most impressive talents is telling you exactly what to do but disguising it as a request.

'I was hoping to give them a tour of the hotel,' Hazel said coldly to her.

'Of course, it has a fascinating history and all the interiors will look beautiful on camera, I'm sure. We can schedule a tour in too, that won't be a problem. Tanya, you have my direct line, don't you?'

Audrey is also very good at not budging.

'Well, then,' Hazel said haughtily, watching Audrey lead Tanya over to shoo away the cameramen and women, 'in that case, Francine, shall we go and enjoy breakfast with Flick and discuss your vision for the show?'

'Lovely.'

'Thomas, if you could prepare our table . . .' Hazel smiled sweetly.

Timothy nodded and I looked up at him apologetically.

'As I'm sure you can imagine, Flick, the world of reality television is extremely competitive,' Francine told me as we took our places at a breakfast table and Timothy swiftly placed napkins on our laps. 'Pilot reality episodes based around the lives of those with stronger public profiles than you have been attempted and failed. If we want yours to succeed, then we have to get it right.'

'Uh, OK.' I nodded.

'Flick is very open to ideas, Francine,' Hazel said as Timothy poured her a fresh orange juice. 'She knows how important this is for her future career.'

'A hotel heiress is a good hook to start, but it won't carry itself. We need drama, we need tears, we need excitement. Just like that viral vlog of yours.' Francine plopped a lump of sugar in her black coffee as it was placed in front of her. 'Do you understand, Flick?'

'I think so.'

'I'm sure you know this already, but Flick is very good friends with Skylar Chase. She's currently in LA but that can be changed. And she's just one of Flick's many high-profile friends, all of whom I'm sure would gladly appear in the show.'

'They would?' I croaked. Hazel shot me a look. 'I mean, they would! Yes. Lots of high-profile pals. They're very glamorous.'

'Fantastic. Now, Tanya mentioned that you live in a flat at the top of the hotel?'

'Yes,' Hazel said, before I could answer. 'But there are many more glamourous suites in the hotel, which I think would suit the aesthetic of the show better. One of them could easily be a substitute as her bedroom.'

'Wonderful,' Francine agreed.

'But it's not my bedroom.'

They both blinked at me.

'Flick, it's not just aesthetic but it's also important we protect your privacy. Being filmed in your actual bedroom might feel quite invasive,' Hazel said in a serious tone. 'Plus, it's a bit small for all the cameras to fit in. Don't you agree?'

'Yeah, I guess so.'

'That's settled, then,' Francine said.

'Did you have any ideas for how you want to structure the episode, Francine?' Hazel asked.

'We really want to introduce the audience to Flick's world: her friends, the hotel, her bubbly personality. We need some fun, interesting events, leading to a big showstopper at the end of the episode with plenty of opportunity for drama. Ah, here come Tanya and Michael.'

They bustled through the dining room to join us, both looking a bit flustered.

'All sorted!' Tanya smiled, taking her seat. 'Francine, I've scheduled in a time for the stock shots. Michael has added it to your calendar.'

'I've also made a list of all the rooms,' Michael added, waving his phone. 'I'll research them this morning and we can work out a plan.'

'Good job,' Francine said. 'Efficient, as ever. We were just discussing ideas for the pilot episode. I always think it's best to just shoot out ideas and see what happens. What do you think?'

'Sounds splendid!' Hazel beamed.

'I'm in.' Tanya smiled too.

'Me too,' Michael enthused.

They all turned to look at me. 'Uh. Me too?'

'Ready?' Francine inhaled deeply, before she began to click her fingers in a staccato rhythm. 'And GO!'

'Flick tries her hand at modelling!'

'Excellent! Contact an agency!'

'Flick goes skiing!'

'Too cold and expensive. Next!'

'Flick records an album!'

'Too obvious. Next!'

'Flick saves the whales!'

'I like that thinking, but tone it down.'

'Flick saves some kittens?'

'Better. Much better.'

'Flick gets a boyfriend!'

I choked on my orange juice at that one and they all looked at me in irritation, as I spluttered all over the place.

'Sorry,' I croaked as Timothy came rushing over to pat me on the back. 'Carry on.'

'How about, Flick hosts a big party for the finale,' Hazel suggested. 'Black tie, ballgowns, socialites and *Tatler* to cover it.'

'Perfect!' Francine cried, before her phone beeped loudly. 'Ah, we have to dash. Excellent work, everyone!'

And in a whirlwind of air kisses, they were suddenly all gone – Hazel had gone to show them out – and I was sitting alone at the table.

'You know what, Timothy?' I said, as I stood up to help him clear the table for the next sitting. 'I can safely say that I have absolutely NO idea what just happened.'

He laughed. 'Me neither, Flick. Not a clue.'

But I didn't care one jot. Because I was getting my own TV show.

And everything was going to be PERFECT.

FIFTEEN

As if things couldn't get any better, the following week Sky arrived in London.

She tried to make it this big surprise by hiding behind one of the giant flower vases in the lobby and jumping out at me when I got home from school, throwing her arms out really wide and screaming 'SURPRIIIIIIIIIIIISE!' at the top of her lungs.

I hated to burst her bubble, but when you're the most famous pop star in the world, it's difficult to get anywhere without someone seeing you. The fact that she'd landed in Heathrow had been all over social media and Grace, who is obsessed with celebrity gossip, had already squealed her head off during morning break and shoved her phone displaying someone's tweet under my nose.

Still, when Sky jumped out, I totally tried to act surprised.

'OH MY GOODNESS, WOW, WHAT A SURPRISE!' I screamed. 'I HAD NO IDEA! WOW! SKY'S HERE, EVERYBODY!'

She dropped her arms as Matthew sniggered behind reception. 'All right. How long have you known?'

'No, no, I had no idea! I'm so shocked!'

'If you're really going to have your own TV show, you're going to have to improve your acting.' She grinned and threw her arms around me. Thanks to her massive high heels, she had to bend down to pull me in towards her. 'How are you?'

'Very busy and important. You?'

'Oh, you know –' she sighed dramatically, running a hand through her thick black curls – 'just trying to come up with a new hit song.'

'I loved your last one.'

'The critics thought it lacked emotion. Maybe I would sing more emotionally if my boyfriend ever bothered to call.'

'I don't know about that but I can tell you the critics are WRONG. Grace and I know all the words. Want me to perform it to you?'

'Who could refuse such an offer?' She smiled gratefully. 'You too busy and important to hang out at some point this weekend?'

'I'll have to check my schedule with my assistant, Fritz. When were you thinking?'

'Saturday afternoon pamper session?'

'I have the school fair.' I rolled my eyes. 'It will be the first day of half-term and the teachers are forcing us to go back to school for it. I've actually volunteered to help out at the cupcake stand.'

She raised her eyebrows. 'They're letting you bake something?'

'Hey! I am an excellent baker!' I protested. 'But don't worry, I'm not in charge of baking the cupcakes, just selling them to raise money.'

Hazel loomed into view behind Sky, with Timothy following behind her carrying several large hat boxes.

'Sky, have you met my aunt? This is Hazel.'

'Actually, your aunt was the one who organised for me to come over,' Sky said, beaming, as Hazel approached us.

'Sky, darling, how is your room?' Hazel asked.

'Perfect, as ever. Flick, is your mom around? I haven't seen her yet and I want to thank her. She left a sweet welcome card on my pillow.'

'Oh, Christine is busy with meetings all day,' Hazel groaned, rolling up the sleeves of her silk coat. 'Work, work, work. That's all she does. I find it highly irresponsible.'

Sky and I exchanged a smirk. I had told her all about Hazel's constant battles with Mum and she had found it hilarious.

'Sky,' Hazel continued, 'the producers of the show are keen to film you coming into the hotel with Flick ready to greet you, so if it's all right with you, we'll film that tomorrow. I'll check what time suits with your assistant but it's likely to be bright and early. Flick has some silly school thing on in the afternoon, even though she's meant to be on half-term. Honestly, the education system these days is a disaster.'

'The school fair; I heard. No problem.' Sky nodded. 'Will it take long?'

'It's just you walking through the door.' I laughed. 'It can't take that long, right?'

WRONG. I was very, very, VERY wrong.

★ ✿ ☾

I discovered that, in TV world, walking through the door doesn't involve someone just walking through a door.

It actually involves:

- Two make-up artists
- A hair stylist
- A clothes stylist
- A five-person-strong camera crew
- Two sound guys

- A director
- A producer and her assistant
- Someone on lighting
- At least one person holding a clipboard but it's unclear why they're there or what they're doing

And HOURS of various takes of Sky walking through the door going, 'Guess who just landed in London?' while I stood there and said, 'Sky! You're here!' over and over and over, until none of the words made sense any more.

'Is it always going to be like this?' I asked, collapsing into one of the velvet-cushioned chairs in the lobby as Sky plonked herself into the other. My feet were killing me in the heels I had been styled in; I could hardly walk.

'Sometimes it's like this on my music videos,' Sky admitted, gratefully taking the bottle of water someone handed her. 'You'd be surprised how long it can take to get these scenes right.'

'That last one was perfect, girls!' Hazel proclaimed, checking her watch. 'Francine has said it's a wrap for today. I'm very proud of you, Flick, well done. You were much more natural in front of the cameras in that last take. The first ones were a bit . . . stiff. I think we'll have to book you in for a massage every morning before you shoot anything; get those shoulders suitably relaxed.'

'I have a new-found respect for reality TV stars,' I said, undoing the strap of my shoe. 'I had no idea it took so much work to look . . . real.'

'Why are you taking off those shoes?' Hazel asked.

'You just said that we were done for today.'

'We're done filming, but that hardly means it's time to get into your pyjamas.'

'I wasn't going to get into my pyjamas, I was just taking off—'

'We're going for lunch and then I've booked us an appointment with Lewis Blume to sort out your wardrobe options for the next few weeks of filming. Excellent publicity for him, of course, but I suppose you owe him one after handbag-gate. Sky, I talked to your assistant and she's pushed back your afternoon meetings, so that you can join us.'

'If you want to,' I added.

'I'd love to.' She smiled. 'As long as I don't have to say the words "guess who just landed in London?" ever again.'

Hazel insisted on taking us to one of the best restaurants in London for lunch, asking Matthew to make the booking. When he reminded her that there was little chance of him being able to get a table there so last minute, she just batted her eyelashes at him and replied, 'Now, Martin, we both know that you have a wonderful ability to pull some strings and get me the best table in town.'

He raised his eyebrows at being addressed as Martin, but said he'd see what he could do and, a few minutes later, he informed us that he'd managed to make the reservation.

'How did you do that?' I asked in admiration when Hazel was chatting to Sky.

He tapped the side of his nose. 'I have my methods.' He glanced over at Hazel as she asked Timothy if he could get her coat. 'Flick, if you're ever uncomfortable with any of this, you do know you can tell me or Audrey. Just say the word and we can get everything back to normal in the blink of an eye.'

'Matthew, why would I want that? Everything was terrible before and now it's brilliant.'

'Oh? It was really that terrible?'

'Don't you remember all the tweets about me on social media? I was the Handbag Hooligan!'

'The what?'

'Never mind, the point is that this show is exactly what I need. It's the perfect opportunity to show everyone who I really am. They'll see that they've got it all wrong.'

'Well, if you're sure. But if ever you have any concerns, you come to me.'

'Thanks, Matthew. And maybe you could drop it in around your son how impressed you are at how motivated and non-diva-like I'm being.'

'I don't think Cal needs me to convince him of that. And anyway –' he smiled, lowering his voice so only I could hear – 'between us, I think Cal always rather enjoyed that dash of diva about you.'

'Come along, Flick!' Hazel called across the lobby. 'Martin, could you get us a taxi?'

I had forgotten what it was like hanging out with someone as famous as Sky, but I was reminded as soon as we stepped into the restaurant. The noise level immediately descended into hushed whispers as we were led through the room to our table and, even though they were trying to be subtle, it was obvious how many camera phones were being pointed in our direction.

The thing is, even if you weren't entirely sure who Sky

was – say, if you'd been living under a rock on Mars or something – you'd definitely be able to guess she was famous just by looking at her. I once laughed my head off when Cal described her as 'radiant' because, seriously, is he an old person. But it was actually quite a good word to sum her up. *She* could definitely pull off a beret.

But then when you're chatting with her, it's also easy to forget she's famous at all. Like at the lunch, when she filled Hazel and me in on the ups and downs of her relationship.

'Sky is dating Prince Gustav Xavier III,' I told Hazel, who looked impressed.

'That charming European prince who Flick attacked?'

'That's the one.' Sky sighed. 'Although I'm not sure I'd describe him as "charming" right now. He barely talks to me.'

'Maybe it's just that he's super busy,' I suggested. 'You know, now that he knows how to work Instagram and stuff. That sort of thing can really take over your day.'

'He's suddenly being distant and I don't know why,' she said quietly. 'I don't know what I've done. And it doesn't help that he's been abroad recently and I've been stuck in the studio working on my new album. I was hoping that coming to London . . . well, I wondered whether he might want to see me.'

'Have you told him you're here?'

'No.' She shuffled in her seat. 'But he'll know. And I don't want to be the one to message first.'

Hazel nodded. 'Well, once he gets in touch, you must invite him to the hotel. We'd love to host both of you for dinner. Perhaps he might even like to appear in the show.'

'I just don't understand why he's avoiding me.' Sky shrugged. 'Maybe he doesn't like my new single either and that's put him off me.'

'Impossible,' I declared, perusing the menu. 'Your song is genius and very catchy. Cal even said so, and you know how picky and pretentious he can be about music.'

'Who's Cal?' Hazel asked, after ordering the lobster.

'Matthew's son,' I informed her and when she looked back at me blankly, I winked at Sky and continued, 'or should I say, *Martin's* son. He goes to my school. You may have seen him hanging around the hotel? You know, thick hair which looks like it has never been brushed, dimples, headphones on, usually carrying some book no one has heard of but he insists is interesting.'

'I can't say I've noticed him,' Hazel said, before turning to Sky. 'We're thinking up ideas for a big black-tie event to film for the pilot. I'll be drawing up the guest list soon, once we've worked out the details, so make sure you put in requests nice and early. I will, of course, include Prince

Gustav. I've heard he's a spectacular dancer.'

I felt weirdly uncomfortable and a bit annoyed at the way Hazel had brushed over Cal, dismissing him so quickly. I didn't want her to think I only wanted celebrities like Sky and Prince Gustav involved in the show.

I pushed my irritation aside, though, and listened to Hazel as she discussed ideas for future episodes, right up until we arrived at Lewis Blume's where he was waiting to greet us at the door.

He ushered us in and Hazel told him that I needed an exciting new, more sophisticated wardrobe. He got to work, instructing us to sit and relax while he put together some pieces with his staff and Hazel took an important phone call outside.

'You know, I could do this more often.' I grinned, settling into the comfortable sofa and ordering a sparkling elderflower.

'Looks like you will be doing this kind of thing all the time for your TV show,' Sky said, sitting opposite me. 'Your aunt has it all planned out for you.'

'Yeah, she's been great. She arrived just in time to save my reputation. I'm just worried the pilot episode won't be good enough and the show won't be commissioned.' I sipped my elderflower while Sky watched me curiously. 'That would be mortifying.'

'It wouldn't at all.' She hesitated. 'You know, Flick, you don't need this TV show to save your reputation.'

I snorted. 'Yeah, because I was doing so well before.'

'Well, let me say, as someone who has been in the spotlight for a while, you don't need an audience to validate what you already know,' she said gently.

I was trying to work out what Sky meant by that when Hazel suddenly came bustling through the door.

'Flick, darling, there's something you should see,' she said, passing her phone to me.

@NancyRose
EXCLUSIVE: Flick Royale of HANDBAG-GATE SCANDAL set to star in reality show about her DIVA DEMANDS! Vlog reaction coming soon!

'Uh-oh,' Sky said, reading it over my shoulder. 'Guess there's no going back now.'

SIXTEEN

Hazel and I were called for an emergency meeting at the hotel with Tanya and Francine.

Waiting in Hazel's suite for them to arrive, I was so nervous I chewed practically all my nails off. Mum was furious that Nancy Rose had got hold of the pilot episode information and, since we got back to the hotel, had been pacing Hazel's suite.

'This wasn't the plan,' she said sharply, directing her comment at Hazel. 'We were only going to film the pilot and then decide on whether or not we'd go ahead with a series.'

'Really, Christine, you're making me feel exhausted with all that walking around,' Hazel said, checking her hair in the mirror. 'Did you really think that we could keep the pilot a complete secret? With all the cameras and a director following Flick around? It would have been impossible, especially with the current press interest in her. You should have seen this coming. And, anyway, who says it's a bad thing?'

Mum just shook her head, muttering under her breath.

Hazel shook her head back at her. 'Don't you have a busy afternoon of meetings to get to?'

'I can cancel them.'

'No need. We have everything covered here and, quite honestly, I don't think your aura is very good for Flick.'

Mum stopped pacing and glared at Hazel. 'My *aura* is just fine.'

'It's all over the place, and what Flick needs now is a calm and serene atmosphere,' she said sternly, walking over to the trolley that room service had brought up and picking up a china teacup and saucer. 'I'll come and find you straight after the meeting and fill you in on everything.'

'Hazel's right, Mum,' I said. 'I don't want you to mess up your day.'

'I can cancel the meetings.'

'Honestly, Mum, it's fine. Hazel and Sky are here, and I know you've got that big presentation in a bit. I'll be fine.' I attempted as sincere a smile as I could.

She sighed. 'All right, then. But I want to hear *everything*. And no decisions made without me, is that clear?'

'Crystal,' Hazel said, stirring sugar into her tea.

Mum gave me a hug and then left the room. As soon as the door closed behind her, I turned desperately to Hazel.

'Do you think Francine and Tanya will be mad?'

'Surely not,' Hazel said calmly. 'Nancy Rose letting the cat out of the bag of course changes the game slightly but I don't see it as a problem.'

'But she's made the show out all wrong,' I complained, as Sky nodded in agreement. 'Why would she say it's about my diva demands?'

'She'll say anything to make it juicier and get more people clicking on her vlog.' Sky sighed, shaking her head. 'How did she even find out about the show? Do you think someone saw us filming this morning and leaked it to her?'

'No, I imagine she got it from her "source",' I said angrily. 'I accidentally let it slip in the school newspaper meeting the other day. I knew Ella would break her promise. Any chance to make me look bad, she'll take it.'

Sky looked confused. 'You think Ella has been feeding Nancy Rose those stories? The girl who was so mean to you last term?'

'We used to be best friends, so every story that Nancy Rose has published Ella has known about. And then as soon as I told Ella about the show, suddenly Nancy Rose has that information too.' I scowled. 'It's a bit too much of a coincidence. Do you think the pilot will be cancelled now?'

'Why on earth would you think that?' Hazel laughed, taking a sip of tea.

'Tanya said when we started that the show might not be picked up by anyone. Now that Nancy Rose has twisted the show to make it sound like it's about a horrible diva, people aren't likely to even give it a chance. They'll turn it down right away.' I slumped back into the sofa, my heart sinking. 'It's over before it's even started and everyone will go on believing I'm someone I'm not.'

'Why don't we wait and see?' Hazel said calmly, putting down her cup and saucer. 'I have a feeling this leak might just work in your favour.'

I looked at her like she was mad. 'How?'

Before she could answer, there was a knock at the door. Hazel rushed over to open it but looked deflated and unimpressed the moment she saw Grace.

'And you are?'

'Grace!' I cried, jumping up and crossing the room to give her a hug as Hazel shut the door behind her. 'What are you doing here?'

'I came over so that we could go to the fair together and Matthew told me you were up here,' she explained. 'He said I should just come straight up. I hope that's OK.'

Sky stood to greet her. Even though they had met at the Hotel Royale Christmas Ball, Grace's eyes still widened in excitement at the sight of her favourite pop star, and when Sky came over to give her a hug, she

159

looked like she might keel over on the spot from the pure joy of it all.

'I saw Nancy Rose's vlog and I wanted to make sure you're all right,' she said to me, once she had pulled herself together after a bout of nervous giggling.

'I haven't even watched the vlog yet. What's it like?'

Grace bit her lip.

'That can't be good,' I groaned, getting out my phone. 'I'll watch it now.'

'Actually, I wouldn't,' Grace advised, plucking my phone from my hands. 'Your show is a really exciting project and you don't need that kind of negativity.'

'So, you don't believe her, then, about all the diva demands? You know the show isn't going to be like that, right? It will show the *real* me,' I said nervously.

Grace blinked in surprise. 'Why would I believe anything Nancy Rose says about you?'

'The more she says these things, the more likely it is people will believe her,' I explained quietly. 'And it doesn't help my case that the stories Ella has leaked to her are true.'

'Francine and Tanya are here, Flick,' Hazel announced happily, marching over from the window. 'I'm so sorry, Gertrude, but Flick's got an important meeting now. So lovely of you to check on her.'

'It's *Grace*,' I corrected, blushing in embarrassment. Luckily Grace appeared to find it amusing. 'And she can stay.' I turned to her. 'If you want.'

'That's all right, I had better get going to the school fair. You're still coming, right?' she asked me before turning to explain to Hazel, 'We volunteered to be in charge of the cupcake stall.'

'How sweet. She'll let you know if she can make it,' Hazel answered. 'It really depends on the meeting.'

Grace nodded. 'Well, hopefully see you later. And Olly texted by the way,' she added at the door. 'He wanted me to tell you that he hopes you're OK too.'

'Thanks,' I said, distracted by Francine and Tanya marching down the corridor towards us. I tried to read their expressions to see if it was bad or good news, but they were both talking frantically into their mobile phones, so it was hard to tell.

'See you, then,' Grace said, waving goodbye and dodging out of the way as Francine brushed past her into the room, hanging up her coat and giving Hazel two air kisses.

'So,' Tanya began, sitting down next to me, 'we've had an overwhelming response.'

'Maybe we can release a statement,' I suggested desperately, looking up at Hazel for help. 'It can explain that Nancy Rose is wrong and that's not what the show is about, and then maybe there might still be hope.'

'Hope?' Tanya looked confused as she typed an email out with impressive speed.

'For the show. It doesn't have to be cancelled.'

Both Tanya and Francine looked up from their phones.

'Why would the show be cancelled?' Francine asked.

'Because . . . I thought because of the emergency meeting after Nancy Rose's tweet . . .' I trailed off.

'Flick, the response has been overwhelmingly *good*,' Tanya explained, her eyes twinkling. 'Right now your show is hot stuff.'

'Hot stuff? Me?' I glanced at Sky. 'Really?'

'Nancy Rose has done us a BIG favour.' Francine nodded, turning her attention back to her phone. 'She's created a great buzz around the project.'

'I thought that might happen.' Hazel beamed, looking as relieved as I felt.

'We wanted to have this meeting to discuss the next steps, publicity-wise. Obviously, we don't yet have as much footage as we'd like—' Tanya said, before Hazel cut in.

'That will of course change now that Flick is on half-term. This week is crucial for filming, and her schedule is completely free,' Hazel told her hastily.

'The camera crew are ready to go for this afternoon,' Francine said, scrolling through a spreadsheet. 'According to the schedule you sent me, Hazel, Flick will be spending the afternoon discussing her holiday to Cannes with a group of vlogger friends. Is that still correct?'

'Huh?' I glanced quizzically at Hazel. 'I'm going to Cannes?'

'Of course!' Hazel laughed. 'And I have a great selection of people you can invite. I'm sure one of them will be available this afternoon to discuss how excited you are about this holiday. Unless you're free now, Sky, to come along?'

'Aren't you helping Grace at the cupcake stall?' Sky asked me.

'Well, I was supposed to be . . .' I replied nervously. I didn't want to let Grace down but I also didn't want to ruin the filming schedule and annoy Francine. 'Maybe we could do both?'

'Darling,' Hazel said, looking pained, 'I highly doubt anyone is going to be interested in your school fair. This is the pilot we're talking about; it has to be outstanding.'

'But then you can meet my friends,' I said, gaining confidence as I realised that volunteering to man the cupcake stand at a school fair was EXACTLY the kind of thing I wanted people to see me doing.

No Handbag Hooligan, bird-hating diva would ever be bothered to help out at a cupcake stall.

Hazel pursed her lips but Tanya was nodding. 'I think a school angle might be quite nice. And it would be good to see some of your school relationships. If you're happy with it, Francine, I'll go ahead and talk to the headmistress about permission to film on school property.'

'Lovely,' she replied, still not looking up from her phone. 'Can you order me a car now too? I'll need to go and scout the area to see what we've got to work with.'

Francine and Tanya stood up to leave, both beginning to make phone calls and telling us they'd see us at the fair as they waltzed out of the room.

'Well, it's not exactly what I had in mind, but I'm sure you know what you're doing,' Hazel remarked, getting out her phone. 'I'll call the stylist and make-up artist up right away. We don't have much time to get you camera-ready.'

I nodded happily, excited for what was to come. I felt a rush at how impressed everyone would be at me helping out at the school fair with an entire camera crew, producer and director. The school students there would know right away that Nancy Rose had got the premise of the show completely wrong and then they could all tweet and Instagram about it.

And this time, there would be no angry pigeons, park

guards or unique designer handbags to get in the way and ruin my EXCELLENT non-diva plan.

I had everything completely under control.

SEVENTEEN

School fairs have always been a big yawn. The only time one was mildly interesting was when Ella and I bought that silly string from one of the stalls and sprayed it all over Mr Grindle's car while he was manning the coconut shy. He threatened to give the whole year detention after half-term if the culprit didn't come forward, so we had to own up, but the two weeks' detention was worth it. You should have seen those ostrich legs run when he came into the car park and spotted the devastation. Ella made me do an impression of it every morning for a week afterwards.

It was weird thinking back on how close I'd thought we were then, when now it felt like she was just waiting for something bad to happen to me so she could help in making me look worse. I guess people change.

Anyway, aside from the silly-string incident, the half-term fairs are pretty uneventful; just a load of stands cobbled together by enthusiastic parents and teachers in a field, or a hall if it's raining, and rubbish funfair music blasting out from the speakers.

Last year, I was passing Mr Hampton as he left the face-painting stand with bright red paint splodged around his face and I'd said very innocently, 'You look cool, Mr H. What are you supposed to be, a ladybird?'

He just looked at me with this really offended expression and replied, 'No, I asked for Spider-Man.'

Which really just sums it all up.

So when I arrived at the gates with a large entourage of camera crew, it understandably caused a bit of a commotion. I spotted the cupcake stand and began to make my way towards it, which took a while due to the shoes I was wearing.

I had tried to tell Hazel that the school fair was a casual vibe, so I wasn't sure heels were a great idea, but she'd insisted.

'Remember,' she'd said, as she pulled out a pair of beautiful strappy shoes and placed them in front of me, 'the dress code is heightened when what you're wearing is going to be broadcast to thousands of viewers. Always better to be overdressed than underdressed. Why do you think reality TV celebrities always look so glamorous all the time? It's because they're dressing for the camera, not for the occasion.'

So I'd taken her advice and, after digging through the bags that Lewis Blume sent over, gone for a loose white

T-shirt tucked into a pair of black ripped skin-tight high-waisted jeans, a trench coat and the green strappy thick-heeled shoes Hazel picked out. When I arrived at the school, Francine and Tanya both agreed I was 'striking the right chord for the sequence', before Tanya suggested some black Wayfarer sunglasses to complete the look.

It wasn't sunny, but that wasn't important.

When I finally reached Grace at the cupcake stand, she was looking at me wide-eyed, with her mouth hanging open.

'Wow,' she said, as the camera crew positioned themselves around me with Francine barking at people about the different angles. 'You look . . . different.'

'Thanks.' I smiled, clapping my hands together. 'I'm excited to help out at the cupcake stand this weekend in my free time! Have you had plenty of customers so far? The cupcakes look delicious!'

'No need to sound so enthusiastic at the moment, Flick,' Hazel informed me from behind the camera crew. 'They're not filming yet.'

'Oh. Well, still, they really do look delicious.'

I walked round to stand next to Grace behind the stand, waiting for Francine to yell 'action'.

'What's going on?' Grace asked, staring at the cameras like a rabbit caught in headlights.

'We're shooting a scene for the pilot episode,' I told her excitedly, as a make-up artist touched up my lipstick. 'As you know, they want to capture the *real* me, so I thought this would be a great opportunity.'

'Oh. Right.' Grace's eyes darted from one camera lens to another. 'What should I do?'

'Just pretend they're not there,' I advised her knowingly. 'Isn't this exciting?'

'I wish I'd dressed up a bit more,' she said, blushing and pulling at her jumper. 'If I'd known I was going to be in your show, I would have made some effort.'

'Don't be silly, Grace, it's called a reality show. You look great as always. It's meant to be real and natural.'

Her eyes flickered to my shoes and then back up to my sunglasses.

'Obviously, I'm a little overdressed.' I grinned. 'But as Hazel said, it's better to be overdressed than —'

'Aaaaaaaaand ACTION!'

Francine's sudden bellow took me by surprise and I stood bolt upright, jolting the table and toppling some of the cupcakes on to the grass.

'Aaaaaaaaand CUT! That was great, people, thank you,' Francine yelled, before turning to have a serious conversation with one of her assistants.

'Wait!' I said, tottering around the stand to Francine as

Grace crouched down to pick up the fallen cupcakes. 'You're not going to use that, are you?'

'Don't worry, Flick,' Tanya cut in, stepping forwards around Francine who didn't look up from her conversation with her assistant. 'That was only one shot. We've got plenty more to do. It's good to get little snippets to use as fillers, that's all.'

'Yeah, but that made me look clumsy,' I explained, patiently. 'And, as Grace here will tell you, I'm not a clumsy person. Right, Grace?'

'Right.' She nodded, standing up to throw the dirty cupcakes in the bin.

But Tanya wasn't listening; she was looking down at her phone which was buzzing in her hand. 'Sorry,' she said, peering at the caller name and then moving away. 'I have to take this.'

'Don't worry, Flick,' Grace said with an encouraging smile. 'I'm sure the next bit they film will be more —'

'Hazel!' I cried, calling her over. 'Hang on, Grace, I just need to ask Hazel something. Hazel, they're not going to use that bit, are they? Did you see? I knocked all the cupcakes to the ground.' I sighed. 'I look like such a clumsy idiot, like in the park with all those pigeons.'

'No, no, you look great!' Hazel assured me. 'Although I think we could do with a little more blush before the next shot. Let me call make-up over.'

I let the make-up artist flurry her brush along my cheeks and the hair stylist spray any loose hairs back into place, and then returned back behind the stand, next to Grace.

'Oh well,' I said, as Grace tried to comb her hair with her fingers. 'I suppose looking clumsy is better than looking horrible.'

'Quiet please!' Francine barked. 'Aaaaaaaaaaand ACTION!'

I smiled broadly at Grace. 'It's so nice to be here with you, Grace, selling cupcakes at the school fair.'

'Uh . . . yeah.' She nodded nervously.

'I hope we sell lots.'

'Um. Me too.'

'It's quite cold, isn't it?'

'Uh. Yes.'

THE WEATHER? I was talking about the WEATHER? I needed something interesting to happen.

As Grace stood tensely next to me, fidgeting with her hair, I waited hopefully for someone to come along and buy a cupcake. But no one was coming near us. Everyone at the fair was standing behind the cameras, watching and whispering to one another.

'Come on over,' I called, waving at some students.

'Come and buy some delicious cupcakes and raise money for charity!'

It was no use. They just stood there, staring, as though we were some kind of circus act.

'Helloooooooooooo!' I cried, waving again. 'Anyone want some cupcakes?'

Out of the corner of my eye, I could see Hazel behind Francine, burying her head in her hands. Francine was shaking her head. This was a disaster.

But then there was a spark of hope as I spotted Cal and Olly over by the second-hand book stall.

'Olly! Cal! Come and buy some cupcakes!'

They stood frozen to the spot as everyone at the fair looked in their direction.

'Come on, guys,' I said, laughing desperately.

But they didn't move.

'Aaaaaaaaand CUT! That was . . . uh . . . well, anyway.' Francine cleared her throat and whispered something in Tanya's ear.

'No, wait,' I said, 'it's OK, those are my friends. They'll come over and buy some cupcakes and you can film me selling some.' I waved madly at Cal and Olly, gesturing for them to join us.

But they just stood there. Why weren't they coming over? What was going on?

I lowered my hand, my face falling.

'I think they're camera-shy,' Grace offered gently.

I felt a lump rise in my throat. 'Why don't they want to support me?'

'Of course they want to support you!' Grace said, looking horrified. 'It's just, we both know that Cal would hate to be in front of a camera. You know he's shy like that. And Olly, well, I don't think it's his thing either.'

'So, he can play a gig to an audience of people but he gets stage fright in front of a couple of cameras? No way,' I said, shaking my head and looking down at the ground. 'I guess they must think as little of me as everybody else does. If I can't even persuade *them* that I'm not an undeserving diva, how am I supposed to persuade the rest of the world?'

'Flick, no, that's absolutely —'

'I'll have a cupcake,' a voice said.

For a moment, I thought I was saved but then I saw who the voice belonged to.

'How much are they?' Ella asked, flicking her hair back. 'Did you make them, Flick? Didn't know you were the baking type but then I suppose recently you have been full of surprises.'

Francine and Tanya stopped their conversation and glanced up with interest.

'No, Ella,' I said through gritted teeth. 'I didn't bake them. And, if you don't mind, we're actually doing some filming for my TV show, so if you could move out of the shot then that would be —'

'You're saying I'm not allowed to buy a cupcake, Flick?' she said shrilly, her voice cutting through the air.

Francine suddenly pulled her headphones back on and signalled to everyone to get into position. Tanya gave me a thumbs up and Hazel, behind her, frantically gestured for me to smile.

This could not be happening. Ella was muscling in on my TV show and making it all about her!

I didn't know what to say, so I didn't say anything at all, pursing my lips and craning my neck to look over her shoulder, desperate for someone else to come along to the stand and rescue me.

'Flick, didn't you hear what I said? Are you ignoring me?' she said, swishing her hair across to the other shoulder. 'Why are you rolling your eyes at me? That's so rude.'

'You know EXACTLY why I am rolling my eyes at you,' I seethed, unable to hold it in. 'Stop playing innocent.'

My eyes flickered towards the blinking red lights on the cameras.

'I don't know what you're talking about,' she replied, putting a hand on her heart as though she was deeply insulted. 'I'm not playing anything. Unlike *some* people.'

The corner of her mouth twitched into a thin-lipped smile.

'Go away, Ella,' I hissed, wishing she would just disappear.

Grace shuffled uncomfortably next to me. 'Um, the cupcakes are only one pound. What colour would you like?'

'I don't know why you're being so mean to me, Flick,' Ella said, picking up a pink cupcake and passing Grace a pound coin. 'I was only trying to buy a cupcake for charity and you ignored me and then told me to go away for no reason at all.'

'That's not true,' I snapped, before taking a deep breath and attempting to keep my tone calm. 'There is a perfectly good reason for me to ask you to leave me alone.'

'Is this because you're annoyed that I got a role on the school newspaper instead of you? I appreciate that you wanted the spot, but it's all fair, Flick. It's not my fault Cal preferred my contribution to yours.'

What?

'Cal doesn't prefer you to me!' I croaked, feeling a sharp stab in my chest as I glanced over at him. 'That's not what happened and you know it!'

'You can't expect to get everything you want handed

to you on a plate. I know you're used to that sort of thing, being who you are, but that's just not real life.'

My jaw dropped.

'You did NOT get a role on the school newspaper instead of me! And I do NOT expect everything to be handed to me on a plate!'

'I think we should just put the whole newspaper thing behind us and make amends, don't you?'

'No, Ella,' I said through gritted teeth. 'I don't!'

She gasped, looking overly stunned, playing up to the cameras. I was so angry that my face and neck were burning up. I tried to catch Hazel's eye to get her to put a stop to the filming but she was engrossed in watching the scene on one of the camera screens.

'You *don't* want to make amends and be friends? Wow, Flick, that's not very nice.'

Hang on. How dare she go out of her way to make me look bad on my OWN SHOW?

I was NOT going to let her get away with it.

'Why would I want to be friends with the person who has been telling LIES about me to the press?' I cried.

Ella looked completely taken aback. HA. There was no chance she could get away with this one. I'd got her and she knew it!

'What are you *talking* about?' she said.

'You know what you've done, Ella,' I spat. 'You know EXACTLY what you've done!'

'Flick, I haven't done anything and you need to calm down because, no offence, but you're acting like a bit of a diva.'

HOW DARE SHE?

'I AM NOT A DIVA!' I shouted, lifting my hands up in exasperation and in the process accidentally tipping a fresh wave of cupcakes to the ground. They scattered everywhere.

Whoops.

'Aaaaaaaaaaaaaaand CUT!'

The film crew all broke out into loud, rapturous applause. I stood frozen in shock as Francine, Tanya and Hazel beamed, clapping along loudly, before launching into excited chatter. The crew lowered the cameras and boom microphones.

'You're not a diva, huh?' Ella sneered, looking at the cupcakes dotted on the grass around the stall. She shook her head at me in disgust and walked off.

'Are you OK, Flick?' Grace asked quietly, putting a hand on my arm.

Seeing everyone's eyes on me as Ella sauntered triumphantly away, I felt a new sense of determination. I wasn't going to let her get in the way of this. It was *my* show.

'You know what, Grace, since handbag-gate, I've put all this effort into trying to make everyone think I'm not a diva and every time it completely backfires. Everything I do to win you all over ends up making me look worse.'

'Flick, none of us think—'

'I'm not going to fight it any more. It's time to try a different tactic. And you know what they say, if you can't beat them –' I readjusted my sunglasses and shot her a winning smile – 'join them.'

EIGHTEEN

I was taking a selfie or two in the lobby when Matthew cleared his throat loudly.

'Flick, what exactly are you doing?' he said, his face looming into view above mine.

'What does it look like I'm doing?'

'It looks like you're lying upside down on a chair in the middle of the reception area.'

He offered me his hand and pulled me into an upright sitting position.

'Matthew, Matthew, Matthew.' I sighed, ignoring the sudden head rush from being upside down so long. 'Achieving the perfect selfie is an art form. I am an artist and this –' I gestured to myself – 'is my canvas.'

'Well, perhaps you would consider moving your *studio* elsewhere.' He smirked. 'The hotel lobby is not the place to hang upside down from a chair taking pictures of yourself.'

'But —'

'No "buts". You're disturbing the guests.' He moved

back round the reception desk. 'Don't you have enough photos of yourself by now? You've been doing nothing else for days.'

'I wouldn't expect you to understand, Matthew. No offence, but this is kind of a young-person thing.'

'No offence taken,' he said with a hint of a smile, rearranging the Hotel Royale pens behind the desk. 'How's the filming going? Seems like you never stop. Will it ever end?'

It was clear after the school fair disaster – or 'cupcake-gate' as it was now known at school – that my exhaustive, persistent efforts to prove to everyone that I wasn't the diva they considered me to be weren't going so well. In fact, they had the exact opposite effect. It was also clear that no matter what I did and how hard I tried, I wouldn't be able to change their minds about me. Nancy Rose and Ella had successfully cemented my image in their brains.

It wasn't worth it.

So, instead of desperately trying to get back in everyone's favour, I'd decided to just leave them to it and embrace my new role as a big TV star.

And it was totally working. Over half-term, I'd done loads of filming, plus I had gained plenty more fans on social media and the number of likes I got were increasing with each post.

'I've been working twenty-four seven,' I told Matthew. 'You know, around school and stuff. There's just been so much going on, and keeping up my social media channels is a full-time job. My followers have rocketed since the series pilot announcement. I have to keep thinking up new ideas for my posts, as well as Fritz's.'

I hesitated.

'Speaking of which, any chance you can get a photo of me sitting on the reception desk answering the phone and doing my lipstick or something? I think that would look really cool. We could do it now when there's hardly anyone around?'

'Nice try, Flick. Never going to happen. The hotel and its property are not your props.'

'Oh well, worth a shot,' I said, leaning on reception. 'I should probably get going anyway, I'm meeting Sky in an hour.'

'Where are you meeting her?'

'Here in the lobby.'

He raised his eyebrows at me. 'And you need an hour to get to exactly where you are standing?'

'No, I have to go get ready for dinner. You know, one needs to *beautify*.' I swished my hair about dramatically, making him laugh.

Audrey emerged from her office holding some files and saw us giggling.

'What are you two up to?' She smiled, handing Matthew one of the files and pointing something out to him. 'Flick, I hope you're not disturbing Matthew.'

'She never disturbs me,' he said with a grin. 'In fact, it's nice to spend some time with her without a camera looming, don't you think, Audrey? These days it's a rarity.'

'Oh, absolutely.'

'It's all in the name of good publicity and not just for me. I specifically asked Francine to get some pretty filler shots of the hotel,' I pointed out, waving happily to a Broadway star, who was currently staying with us, as he crossed the lobby. He'd done a clip for my Instagram the other day of him teaching me to tap dance in the music room. It had got HUNDREDS of likes.

'I preferred it when we had less publicity and fewer cameras,' Audrey said, checking something on the reception computer. 'I don't know how you can possibly enjoy it.'

'What are you talking about? It's great!'

Which was mostly true.

Obviously, there were some *tiny* disadvantages to being followed by cameras everywhere. For example, it took me a hundred years to get ready these days because

I had to make sure my make-up was absolutely perfect and my hair was styled before I went anywhere. Even a natural look could be pretty tiring to create. Since having a make-up artist on hand, I had really come a long way with my contouring and fake-eyelash application skills.

Then there was the matter of clothes. Lewis Blume was a firm favourite, but since Nancy Rose's exclusive vlog about the show pilot, a load of other designers had sent me their clothing samples too, hoping to get them on TV, which was GREAT, but also made it very hard to choose what to wear each day, so that took a while.

After the huge stress of just getting ready to leave my bedroom in the morning, I also had to make sure that throughout the day I was posting pictures often enough to keep my new fans updated, hoping every time I checked my latest post that the number of likes and views were increasing. Which was actually very tiring.

And, as much as I liked the crew, they could get a bit annoying. Sometimes I didn't know where I was going or what I was doing each day, and then Francine would boss me around all the time and tell me to pronounce something better than how I was saying it.

I had to hang out with a bunch of people I had never met before at posh events where nothing actually happened, and it was hard to have proper conversations with friends like Sky when the cameras were around, capturing our every move.

I was also falling behind with my homework because whenever I got any free time to myself, I actually just wanted to collapse on my bed, like the other day when I was so tired that I lay on the sofa in a complete daze and watched Fritz bark at a pigeon sitting on the windowsill for at least half an hour.

But other than those tiny points, it was brilliant.

'Each to their own, I suppose,' Audrey concluded. 'But I, for one, will be glad when this pilot episode is done and dusted, the cameras are gone and Hazel is back in New York.'

'Audrey,' Matthew said, shooting her a warning look.

'I'm just saying –' she shrugged, lowering her voice – 'her outlandish requests can be time-consuming. It's a busy time of year.'

'It's always a busy time of year at Hotel Royale. And no request from any guest is ever too much trouble,' Matthew stated, throwing back his shoulders proudly.

'All right, Employee of the Century.' Audrey smiled, rolling her eyes. 'Enough of the soundbites.'

'Hazel won't be leaving any time soon, especially if a whole series gets commissioned,' I informed them. 'And, anyway, we still need to film the big finale. It's going to be a black-tie do in the ballroom. I'm trying to think up ideas to make it a bit different – do you guys have any thoughts? Do you think a masquerade ball would be too much? Or is that cool?'

'Have you asked Cal?' Matthew said cautiously. 'Or Grace and Olly? They might have some ideas.'

I raised my eyebrows at him. 'Why are you giving me that look?'

'What look?' he replied innocently, as Audrey smiled to herself. 'I'm not giving you any look.'

'Yes, you are.'

'I just heard on the grapevine that you haven't spent much time with your friends recently.'

'Let me guess, does the grapevine happen to be Cal-shaped?' I shook my head.

'I've noticed he's been a bit down lately too.' Matthew paused. 'You wouldn't happen to know why?'

I shrugged. 'Maybe his shiny new friend Ella isn't as sparkly as he thought she was.'

'Ah.' He shared a look with Audrey.

'It's not a big deal. I'm busy filming and they've got lots to do with the newspaper and stuff. They wouldn't want me around anyway.'

'That's not true, I'm sure,' Audrey insisted. 'Cal keeps coming to the hotel looking for you.'

'He does?' I narrowed my eyes at her. 'When?'

'He came here a lot during half-term. And he's been here recently a few times after school,' Matthew replied. 'Every time, you've been out filming. He mentioned you hadn't been hanging out as much at school either.'

'I haven't been *ignoring* him,' I pointed out. 'I've just not been as talkative. I've got lots on my plate.'

'Are you sure you're not still holding a grudge against him and Olly for what happened at the school fair?' Audrey asked curiously.

'All he had to do was come and buy a cupcake,' I muttered. 'But nooooooo, he rejected my pleas for him to come over, then he let Ella step up and we all know how that turned out.'

'I get it, Flick, but I think it's time you forgave him, don't you?' Audrey said gently. 'You may love being on camera, but not everyone does.'

'If there'd been no cameras around and it had just been you,' Matthew began, 'he would have been first in line. I know that for a fact.'

'Why don't you pop him a message?' Audrey suggested, picking her files up and heading back to her office. 'Or, better yet, talk to him at school tomorrow.'

'I'll consider it,' I said with a sniff, as Matthew nodded,

looking satisfied with the outcome. 'But that does NOT mean I forgive him.'

FINE. I forgive you

???

I mean, good evening, Cal.
How are you?

Who is this?

Excuse me?

I don't have this number saved

IS THIS A JOKE?!

No? Seriously, who is this?

It's Flick, you moron!

Flick Sprogg? Wow! It's been years!
How are you? Are you still building with Lego?

WHO ON EARTH IS FLICK SPROGG?!
AND WHY IS SHE BUILDING WITH LEGO?

I'm sorry, I'm lost. This isn't Flick Sprogg
from the East Anglia Summer Camp 2012?

NO, THIS IS NOT FLICK SPROGG
FROM THE EAST ANGLIA SUMMER
CAMP 2012

Oh! What a shame. Flick Sprogg was
really very talented at building Lego. It
would be nice to reconnect. So, if you're
not Flick Sprogg, who are you?

HOW MANY FLICKS DO YOU KNOW,
BONEHEAD?

Well, there's Flick Sprogg from the East
Anglia Summer Camp 2012 and then . . . hmmm,
nope, can't think of any others

You think you're so funny, don't you?

I've heard I'm a hoot

That's not a word

"a hoot (noun, informal): an amusing situation or person" Direct quote from the dictionary

I meant, that's not a word people actually USE

So, you've missed me, huh?

WHAT?

That's why you're texting me. You've missed your old buddy, Cal

I have NOT missed you. And don't use the word "buddy"

Sure

If you must know, Audrey and your dad told me I ought to message you, that's all. To forgive you and stuff. They felt sorry for you

If you say so

They DID!

Yup. Sure

It's true!!!! Ask them!

You missed me

I DID NOT MISS YOU. Ugh, why did I bother texting you?

Feel free to stop whenever you like

Fine

Hard, isn't it?

What is?

Not messaging me

It's really easy actually.
I'm very busy

See? There you go again,
messaging me

BECAUSE YOU MESSAGED ME

And again!

I retract my earlier statement about
forgiving you. Goodbye

No worries, I'm going to track down
Flick Sprogg and be friends with her

THERE IS NO FLICK SPROGG

There is too. We built a raft together out of sticks when we were on the East Anglia Summer Camp 2012. Does that make you jealous?

WHY would I be jealous about building a raft out of STICKS??

They were more like logs really. We used barrels too. They were blue

I don't CARE about the raft

Flick Sprogg was particularly nifty with ropes, I remember

Stop messaging me please

I'm so happy we're friends again

We're not friends

Life can be a lonely abyss without a friend to lean on in times of trouble

192

Go away, please

In the words of Simon and Garfunkel . . .

Who???

"Old friends, old friends,
Sat on their park bench, like bookends"

WHAT ARE YOU EVEN SAYING?

Thank you for admitting that you have missed me. That took great courage. May you have a peaceful slumber and awaken fulfilled in the knowledge and acceptance of your honesty

I hate you

NINETEEN

I was finding it VERY hard to concentrate at school. Firstly, I was exhausted from having no downtime ever; secondly, I couldn't make myself feel all that motivated when I knew that as soon as the pilot got picked up, I probably wouldn't need to go to school any more because my career would be all set up and ready to go; and thirdly, because everywhere I looked I saw Ella.

I really thought after the whole cupcake saga, she might BACK OFF but, like Fritz when he hears any kind of food wrapper rustling, she continued to linger.

The difference is, Fritz is very much welcome and adorable to look at, even when drooling. Ella is not. (Welcome, I mean. I have no idea what she looks like when she's drooling, but I'm going to guess it's not that adorable.)

I kept seeing her chatting away to Cal in the corridors in between lessons, and after school sometimes they would walk together to their newspaper meetings. She was even closer at lunchtimes now as she'd moved from her usual canteen table to the one right behind ours. I asked Grace if she'd noticed that and she just shrugged and said it was probably because the table behind ours was further from the door, so didn't have that draught.

I knew that I couldn't avoid her completely because we went to the same school, but it was very difficult to focus on all the good, harmonious things in my life and move on from the negative things when Ella was constantly in my line of sight.

At least there hadn't been any more tweets about my life from Nancy Rose, now that I had called Ella out on that at the school fair. But still, it felt as though she was constantly in my way.

For example, the morning after I texted Cal forgiving him for deserting me at the fair, I saw him sitting on the school steps, reading some nerdy book, and I couldn't stop myself smiling as I headed towards him.

I would never say it out loud, but I *had* kind of missed hanging around with him and putting up with his odd sense of humour and mischievous grins with those silly dimples.

But then I stopped in my tracks.

Because he'd looked up and grinned with those silly dimples, not at me, but at the person who'd sidled up to him from nowhere and sat down, producing some photos for him to look at.

Ella.

I watched her pointing at the photos while he nodded and laughed along. It felt as though someone had punctured my stomach and I was deflating slightly.

'Hey, Flick, you OK?'

I started at Olly's voice in my ear, realising that I was just standing right in the middle of the yard, staring at Ella on the school steps.

'Yeah, yeah, I'm fine,' I said, blushing. 'How are you?'

'I'm good. It's rare that you're not rushing somewhere or with a bunch of people, so I thought I'd take the opportunity to come and talk to you.' He smiled.

'Yeah, I guess it's all been a bit . . . crazy lately,' I admitted. 'Where's Grace?'

'Nestled away somewhere on her laptop, probably the library,' he informed me, as we began to walk together towards the school building. 'She's been very dedicated to her investigative research recently.'

'Oh?' I replied, trying hard not to look anywhere near where Cal and Ella were as we passed them on the steps. I noticed she was showing him pictures of HERSELF modelling her accessorising of the school uniform.

'Grace is working on a secret project, but she won't tell us what it is. When I asked her to give me a clue, she said she wanted the truth once and for all.' Olly laughed, rolling his eyes. 'Make of that what you will.'

'That's strange. She hasn't mentioned it to me.'

He held open the door for me and I noticed a group of girls clustered on the school steps watching us enviously.

'You haven't exactly been around for her to mention it.' He shrugged, strolling down the corridor towards my locker. 'You've been so busy with the filming, we've hardly seen you.'

'I was telling Matthew the other day, it really is a full-time job.'

'The pilot episode must be nearly done by now,' he said, leaning on the locker next to mine.

'Yeah,' I said with a smile. 'It would be nice to have a break.'

He raised his eyebrows. 'Until filming starts for the full series, hopefully, though, right?'

'Right. Yeah. Exactly.'

I felt him watching me closely but I couldn't bring myself to look him in the eye. It wasn't that I didn't want to film a full series, I mean, that would be MAD. It was tiring and, yeah, I missed just slobbing about with friends, BUT I had to stay focussed on the long game. This show was the key to . . . how did Hazel describe it? My glittering career.

Yeah. That was it.

'Are you still coming to the gig tomorrow night?'

I blinked up at him, lost in my thoughts. 'Sorry?'

'The gig?' Olly prompted. 'You know, the emerging bands one. It's tomorrow night.'

'Oh! Right, yeah, of course. Your gig. Yeah, course I'll be there.'

'Really? You don't have any dramatic scenes to film involving cupcakes or anything?' he teased, smiling broadly.

'Ha ha, very funny.' I sighed, rolling my eyes. 'Not that I'm aware of.'

'Good.' He grinned. 'I'll be looking for you in the audience, then. The bands have to be there early for sound testing and stuff, but I think Cal, Grace and Ella are going to meet at ours beforehand and head over together so you should check timing with them.'

'OK, sounds good, I'll . . . hang on . . .' I paused midway through opening my locker. 'Did you just say Cal, Grace and *Ella*?'

'Yeah.' He nodded, looking a bit sheepish.

'Ella is going to your gig? Since *when*?'

'It came up the other day in an editorial meeting

and she was asking questions about it, so Cal said she should come along.'

'*Cal*?' My mouth went dry as I tried to get my head round this new information. 'Why would he do that? Why would he want *her* there?'

'I think he thought it would be quite a nice team-bonding thing,' Olly said. 'Anyway, I'm glad you're coming; it should be a fun night. Unless we muck up all our songs, in which case, not so much fun. Although, potentially more entertaining for you.'

I was so stunned as I pulled open my locker, I forgot to use my arm as a blocker for the mountain of stuff I had in it and it suddenly came tumbling out at full force, scattering everywhere all over the floor.

'Seriously, Flick,' Olly said, laughing, 'you have GOT to tidy your locker.'

He bent down to help me pick everything up, while my brain whirled. I think, until then, it had bugged me that she was on the newspaper team and everything, but I'd felt relatively safe in the knowledge that as soon as the issue was done and dusted, things would go back to normal and she would never speak to any of us again.

But this was a whole new level. Cal didn't just have to hang out with her, he *wanted* to.

Suddenly I had a pounding headache.

When Olly and I had gathered all my books and papers into a neat pile on the floor, I scooped it up in my arms and shoved it back into my locker, pushing it in and shutting the locker door quickly before it could all fall out again.

'You missed one,' Olly said, bending down to get a notebook I hadn't seen behind me. 'Here.'

'Thanks.'

As I took it from him, I noticed he held it slightly longer than was necessary so our fingers brushed.

'I'm really glad you'll be there tomorrow, Flick,' he said, his dark intense eyes looking straight into mine. 'We've missed having you around.'

TWENTY

'A gig?'

Hazel blinked blankly at me, putting down her glass of Champagne.

'What do you mean a *gig*?'

'You know, people playing the guitar, people singing, someone on drums. That kind of thing,' I explained while I tried to make Fritz stay still. It was hard to put him in his pyjamas when he kept wriggling.

'I can't think of anything worse!' She hesitated, turning to smile sweetly at Sky. 'Apart from your concerts, of course, which I'm sure are marvellous.'

'Thanks, Hazel.' Sky laughed, eating cookie-dough ice cream straight from the tub. 'Mine are pretty awesome.'

Mum was at a conference, so Hazel and Sky had come up to discuss last-minute details for next week's ball, although I'd had no say in anything whatsoever. Hazel had organised everything, even the charity we were raising money for, which I really appreciated, although it would have been nice to at least have been asked.

I wanted to throw the ball in honour of a dog charity, as that would please Fritz greatly.

But I didn't want to kick up a fuss and sound ungrateful for all the hard work Hazel had done, so I figured I would leave it and maybe when we got round to filming the second episode, I could pitch a dog charity event.

And I'd had to beg Hazel to let all my school friends come, reminding her that I hardly knew anyone else she'd included on the guest list. She'd eventually relented.

'It's a gig for new and upcoming bands,' I told them, doing up Fritz's buttons.

'Let me get this straight,' Hazel said, with a horrified expression. 'These bands aren't even signed? They might be awful!'

'They've been selected. And I've heard Olly's band play before, they're really good.'

'I don't know, Flick, this hasn't been scheduled.'

'Well, I've now scheduled it,' I said, firmly. After being told what kind of ball I was hosting and who I was throwing it for, I had to put my foot down about *something*.

'All right, then.' Hazel sighed. 'I'll give Tanya and Francine a call, and I'm sure it won't be a problem getting passes for all the camera crew. Though I hardly think the lighting will be —'

'No camera crew,' I interrupted. 'I don't want to do any filming.'

'But Flick —'

'Hazel, I don't want to sound ungrateful but I really could do with some time off from having a camera in my face and being told what line to say a hundred times, and where to sit and where to stand. Besides, Cal and Olly have already made it very clear how they feel about being on camera. Remember their refusal to come near them at the school fair?' I took a deep breath. 'I just want a night with some friends. No cameras.'

She pursed her lips. 'All right, then. No cameras. I doubt it will be of any interest for the pilot anyway. You are baffling, though, Flick. Why would you want to spend your evening listening to bands that aren't good enough to have been signed by a record label?'

'Hey,' Sky said, rolling her eyes, 'everyone has to start somewhere. I played plenty of gigs before I got signed.'

'Plus, I owe it to Olly to go. I have to cheer him on and I said I'd be there ages ago. And I also have to go because . . .' I hesitated. 'Never mind.'

Sky furrowed her brow, lowering the ice-cream tub. 'What were you just about to say?'

'Huh?'

'You were about to say something. Another

reason why you want to go to this gig.'

'Nope, no other reason.' I reached for Fritz's slippers, popping them on to each of his paws. 'OK, Fritz, you're all ready for a good snooze.'

He yawned and stretched, plodding over to his basket.

Sky narrowed her eyes at me. 'Fliiiiiiiiick?'

'OK, FINE.' I heaved a great sigh. 'Ella is going. With Cal.'

Sky looked taken aback. 'What?'

'Ella? Who is Ella?' Hazel asked.

'Cupcake girl,' Sky explained.

'Ohhhhh,' Hazel said. 'That Ella.'

'Yes, that Ella. Somehow they've all become friends because she's deluded them all into thinking she's a nice person and I'm a horrible one. And so I have to go to show them that I'm way more a supportive friend than she is.'

'You're jealous,' Sky announced, picking the ice cream back up again.

'PLEASE! I am not jealous of Ella. She's on a stupid school newspaper editorial team, while I have my own TV show. If anyone is jealous, it's her.'

'Uh-huh.' Sky nodded knowingly. 'If you say so.'

'I thought you didn't like Ella,' Hazel observed, picking up her drink. 'Won't there be a few fireworks if you show up to this gig, just like all that drama at the school fair?'

'Nope, because I've got a buffer.'

'A buffer?' Hazel looked curious. 'As in, a nail buffer?'

'No. As in, a person buffer. I'll have someone with me to make sure that no diva-style drama happens; someone to look after me and make sure I'm on my best behaviour; someone so brilliant and amazing that no one will be paying any attention to me at all.'

'I'm flattered, darling.' Hazel smiled. 'But I don't think a gig is up my street.'

'No offence, Hazel, but I was actually talking about Sky.'

'Me?' Sky said, with a mouth full of cookie dough, while Hazel looked mildly insulted. 'You want me to come to Olly's gig tomorrow night?'

'Yes, I do. If you're available.'

She nodded thoughtfully. 'Yeah, I'm available. I haven't heard from Gustav all week so I think that vague plan we made to see each other this weekend is off the cards.'

'You guys still haven't spoken?'

'Nope. I'm trying not to think about it too much.'

'I'm so sorry, Sky.'

'Does it count as a break-up if they never call you to break up, they just . . . stop calling?'

'I can't believe Prince Gustav would do that,' I said, shaking my head. 'He was so smitten with you.'

'He's been distant for a while. I should have known this was coming. Anyway, I'm in London so I'm running with that British attitude – stiff upper lip and all that. A gig tomorrow night sounds good,' she said with a brave smile. 'Something to look forward to.'

★ ❀ ☽

Walking into the concert, I was so relieved I had Sky by my side. All day I'd felt weirdly anxious about it and, during the car journey on the way to the venue, I realised that my hands were seriously clammy, which was gross.

'Don't worry,' Sky said, noticing me biting my lip as we walked through the doors into the room full of bustling people, 'I won't let Ella say anything mean to you. If she wants to see real diva behaviour, I'd be very happy to oblige.'

I laughed. 'Thanks, Sky. But don't worry. I'm determined there will be no drama tonight, even if that means being nice to Ella.'

It wasn't long before people started doing double takes and nudging each other, as Sky glided through the room next to me. We made our way towards Cal, Ella and Grace, who were right in the middle of the room.

'Hey,' I said cheerily, when we reached them. 'We haven't missed Olly, have we?'

'Hey, you're here!' Cal smiled. 'No, they haven't been on yet. You haven't missed anything.'

Grace squealed and pulled me into a hug. 'Olly will be so pleased you made it.'

'Of course I made it. And I hope it's OK that I brought along a friend.'

Sky came forwards to give Grace a hug and, while Grace rambled on about how she couldn't believe Sky remembered her name, and would there be any chance of getting a couple more selfies, I stood awkwardly next to Cal and Ella.

I noticed Ella's expression had soured the minute I arrived, so I decided to try to break the ice a little bit, just so she knew that I didn't want any tension.

'I like your outfit, Ella,' I said, nodding at her black silk top and ripped jeans. 'You look really nice. And are you wearing the raspberry lip gloss?'

She hesitated, looking thrown off guard, before saying, 'The strawberry one.'

'It really suits you.'

'Thanks.'

Luckily the lights went down at that moment for the first band to come on to the stage, so I didn't have to attempt any further conversation but, as everyone started clapping, I caught Cal's eye.

He was looking at me with that familiar, mischievous grin. I hadn't seen it in a while and at first I felt elated but then I realised why he was smiling. I had made an effort with the girl he liked. Any happiness I felt seeped right on out of me at that thought.

There were three bands playing before Olly's came on and, as I bopped along to their songs, I noticed that Cal smelled really good and it made me want to bop a bit closer to him, just to keep smelling him.

Which, when I think about it, is the creepiest thing that's ever crossed my brain.

But one of the times that I was bopping a little closer in order to smell him, my arm brushed against his arm and then my body completely tensed up because I was so aware of it, and Grace turned round just at that moment and went, 'You know, Flick, when you sway, you look a little bit like a penguin.'

Which was mortifying.

I decided I couldn't let Cal and Ella get me down, especially when I was here for Olly, so I made sure I was whooping and cheering along with the others as enthusiastically as possible when Olly's band came on stage.

That's when I thought I saw Tanya out the corner of my eye.

As Olly announced the name of the song, I looked directly at the spot where I thought I'd seen her and she wasn't there, so I decided I was going mad. I shook my head and then cried, 'GO, OLLY!' at the top of my lungs.

He heard and searched the crowd with his eyes, squinting into the spotlights, eventually finding me and breaking into a wide smile.

I have to admit, the stage lighting really did work wonders for those perfect cheekbones.

They started up their first song and I was keeping myself busy, admiring Olly's cheekbones, when I saw Tanya again. I looked over immediately. I gasped. I wasn't imagining it.

Tanya was here at the gig. Next to her was Francine. And they were leading a bunch of cameramen, pushing their way through the crowd, trying not to knock anyone out with their equipment.

'No,' I whispered, as Tanya spotted me and pointed me out to Francine. 'No, no, no.'

I poked Sky in the back and she turned round, grinning. 'Hey, Olly is really good. This song has a lovely melody.'

'*They're here,*' I hissed.

She followed my gaze and her mouth fell open when she saw them.

'Oh my God. What are you going to do?'

'They have to leave,' I said angrily. 'I'll try to get them to go without causing too much of a scene.'

I slipped away from Cal and elbowed my way through the audience to stop the TV crew in their path, but I was too late. By the time I reached them, they'd got in so many people's way with all their cameras and sound booms, that some of the crowd were starting to boo and shout at them.

'Tanya, what are you doing here? You have to leave!' I begged.

Tanya clearly realised that there were too many people and it was too noisy to attempt any filming, so she started instructing everyone to turn back, but it was so rammed, it was causing an even bigger commotion to go back the way they came. One woman got hit in the head with a sound boom and when the sound guy swung the boom microphone away from her, apologising profusely, he managed to hit four more people on the head in doing so. Meanwhile, the few people who weren't annoyed by the crew's presence, were jumping in front of the cameras and crying, 'Film me, film me! Hi, Mum!'

Four security men pushed their way towards us and began instructing Francine to get out of there, while she yelled at them to clear the floor so that her crew could set up properly, insisting that she had the organiser's permission to film.

'Francine,' I said, firmly. 'You all need to leave! I refuse to film here!'

'Flick,' Cal's voice said in my ear, as he came to help. 'You have to get them out of here. They're ruining Olly's performance!'

'I'm trying! Cal, I swear I didn't arrange for them to come – you have to believe me,' I pleaded, hoping he could hear me over all the booing and shouting.

He didn't have the chance to reply, as the boom microphone came swinging towards him and he had to duck quickly, before yelling to the sound guy, 'Seriously, why can't you just hold it steady?'

I was so busy telling the crew to get out and so mixed up in the complete chaos they had brought, that I hadn't noticed that the band had stopped playing until the crew were finally almost all out of the door.

I turned to look up at the stage and Olly was shaking his head miserably at me, as the other band members looked at each other, not sure what to do.

'You need to leave,' a security man told me gruffly, his

instruction echoing through the muffled silence of the venue. 'Now.'

I did as I was told, pushing through the door into the cold night air, everyone's accusing eyes watching me go.

TWENTY-ONE

I had just opened the bag of chocolate buttons when a voice came out from the darkness behind me.

'Flick.'

I screamed and the bag flew into the air, scattering its contents everywhere.

'Stop doing that!' I hissed at Mum as she clasped a hand over her mouth, giggling. 'Chef still hasn't forgiven me for last time. He noticed a couple of bags were missing, you know.'

'I know.' She laughed, strolling to the cupboard and pulling out the dustpan and brush. She held them out for me. 'He didn't believe me when I said it was Matthew. No idea why. I'll let you do the honours while I fish out another bag.'

I swept up the chocolate and poured it into the bin, before padding back across the kitchen in my slippers to slide down next to Mum, who was now sitting with her back against the baking cupboard, happily digging into another bag of buttons.

'So,' she began, as I nibbled the chocolate, 'I heard the gig the other night was eventful.'

'I do NOT want to talk about it.'

'That bad, huh?'

'The worst.' I hugged my knees to my chest. 'Somehow, in trying to make everything better, I've managed to make everything worse.'

'Everyone in the world feels that way sometimes,' she said, 'trust me.'

'Yeah, but I've really screwed up.' I took another button. 'I don't have any friends left.'

'I happen to know that's not entirely true. Apparently, you and Sky enjoyed some room service during a movie night yesterday.' She raised her eyebrows. 'A little birdie told me that you requested five tubs of ice cream?'

'Chef is such a telltale,' I huffed, rolling my eyes. 'We weren't sure what flavour to get. And it was an emergency.'

'Wise choice just to order them all, then.'

After the eventful night at the gig, plus given her current relationship status, Sky had declared that a movie night with as much ice cream as possible was an absolute necessity. Halfway through the first movie, her phone had beeped.

'It's Gustav!' she said with a gasp.

'What does he say?' I had asked, eagerly.

She read the text. 'He wants to meet.'

'Are you going to go?'

She had picked at the cushion thoughtfully. 'Yeah. I think so. I guess it's important to get closure.'

'Closure. Right.' I had nodded. 'How American.'

She had thrown the cushion at me and declared that we weren't allowed to talk about Prince Gustav OR the gig for the rest of the evening. But I couldn't stop thinking about how I'd ruined everything with my friends. I'd been too embarrassed to message or call any of them, so I'd just turned off my phone. When I had turned it on this morning with a sense of hope, my heart sunk. No new messages.

'I think it's just confirmed everything I hoped it wouldn't,' I told Mum, after filling her in about what went down at the gig.

'What's that?'

'That I'm not a good person, after all,' I said quietly. 'That I'm just a spoilt, silly diva, who fights people over designer handbags and knocks over cupcake stalls in a strop. That I don't deserve to be on the "50 Heirs to Watch" list. You should have seen Olly's face when I ruined his band's performance. I don't think he'll ever talk to me again.'

'He'll come round. They all will. Give them time.' She

wrapped her cardigan closer round her. 'Nobody's perfect, Flick. You didn't know the camera crew were going to show up; once things have calmed down, your friends will understand that.'

'I guess.' I hesitated. 'Mum?'

'Yeeeeees?'

'Can I tell you a secret?'

She smiled. 'I'm listening.'

I took a deep breath before blurting out, 'I'm not sure whether I like being a reality TV star.'

She raised her eyebrows. 'Really?'

'I know it seems crazy but I've been thinking about it, and these last few days when they haven't been around . . . I haven't missed them at all. In fact, I've felt relieved.'

She didn't say anything, so I decided I should carry on and the next thing I knew, I'd launched into a gigantic speech, rattling everything off my chest before I could stop myself.

'I thought that doing this TV show would show everyone the real me but instead, doing this show has made me more confused than ever about who the *real* me really is! And I hate all those stupid cameras always being in my face, making me feel self-conscious about every single movement I make. You can't talk about proper stuff in front of them, and then Francine makes you repeat the same sentence over and over and over until none of it is real any more but, according to them, it's *more* real. Which doesn't make ANY sense. And Fritz is stropping more often because I do more Instagram posts about me than of him, and I don't have time to take him on as many walks any more, and when we do go on walks, we can't go to his favourite park because they don't have permission to film there, so we have to go to a stupid park where there aren't any squirrels for him to bark at, just a load of posh flower beds and varnished benches.'

I paused for breath.

'And my feet hurt from the shoes.'

'The shoes?'

'Sometimes I have to change my shoes a few times a day, as well as my outfits, to make it look like we're filming on different days. It gives the appearance that you're filming over a longer period of time than you are,' I explained. 'And new shoes always rub. My feet are completely torn up.'

'Oh.' Mum exhaled. 'I never thought about that.'

'Yeah, well, spare a thought for my paws.' I wiggled my toes in my slippers. 'I've ruined everything, haven't I?'

'No, you haven't,' Mum said gently, reaching out to tuck a lock of my hair behind my ear.

'You have to say that because you're my mum.'

'Maybe a little,' she said, putting her arm round me and drawing me towards her.

'I wish I didn't have to host this stupid ball.' I sighed. 'But the invitations have all gone out and everyone's put so much effort into it. It's a bit too late to cancel it. It's ridiculous. I'm throwing a charity ball but I didn't have any say in the guest list and I didn't have any say in the charity that we're throwing the ball for in the first place.'

Mum looked thoughtful.

'And the only people I really want to come probably won't because I messed everything up,' I added. 'I've ended up disappointing everyone.'

There was a moment of silence and then Mum spoke.

'Do you remember years ago when I got you that dinosaur toy?'

'A *dinosaur* toy? Are you mixing me up with Cal?'

I felt a stab in my stomach at the thought of Cal. I hated the idea that he was thinking badly of me right now. He must be so disappointed. Ella was probably with him right at that moment, telling him that she'd told him so about me.

'No, it was definitely you.' She laughed. 'You loved it, you brought it everywhere with you around the hotel. A really famous actor at the time who was having afternoon tea saw you with it and asked if he could take a look at the dinosaur. And do you know what you said?'

'Um, something along the lines of, "This is Cal's lame toy, not mine, please don't judge me"?'

'You said, "It's not a dinosaur, it's a dragon." And after a while, the actor nodded and said, "Ah yes, I see now that it is a dragon."'

She looked at me meaningfully, as though she'd just imparted some kind of ancient wisdom. I stared blankly back at her.

I literally had no idea what she was harping on about.

'Is there meant to be a point to this story? Or are you just doing that random thing parents do where they talk about nostalgic childhood stuff for no reason at all?'

'What I'm trying to say is,' she said, pausing for a deep breath, 'you can see something a different way. Turn it into something else.'

There was a long, drawn-out silence. Mum raised her eyebrows at me.

'You still don't get it, do you? I'm going to have to spell it out.'

'Well, no offence, Mum – I appreciate this could have been a really magical, movie moment, but you're not making it easy with all your cryptic talk.'

'Make everything better by doing things your own way!' she cried in exasperation. 'You've got this ball lined up and you can't cancel it now. So, turn it into whatever you want it to be.'

'Ooooooooooh.' I nodded. 'I see. You didn't make that very clear.'

'That was exhausting,' she huffed, leaning back against the cupboard and closing her eyes.

'It is 2 a.m.,' I pointed out. 'We should probably go to bed.'

But when I got back to bed, I didn't get much sleep. Because I was working out a genius plan to make everything better again.

It was time to turn the dinosaur into a dragon.

TWENTY-TWO

I bought Grace a tortoise.

Well, I meant to buy her a tortoise. I actually ended up buying her a terrapin. Which turned out to be a turtle.

So, it wasn't a great start to my heartfelt apology.

'A companion for your tortoise, Bruce!' I exclaimed, standing on hers and Olly's doorstep with the glass tank. 'And he's all yours.'

She blinked at me. 'This is for me?'

'Yeah! As a sorry. For ruining the other night and also for not being there for you lately. I hope this is a start to making things up.' I nodded at the tank. 'I've just been calling him "Tortoise", you know, for ease, but feel free to come up with a more imaginative name.'

'Um, Flick?' Grace said, taking the tank. 'You know this isn't a tortoise, right?'

'What?'

'This isn't a tortoise.'

'How can it not be a tortoise?'

'Because it's a turtle.'

'It's a WHAT?'

'Didn't you think it was weird that it was in water?'

'Why would that be weird?'

'Because tortoises are land creatures.'

'I can't believe this!'

'What's going on?' Olly said, suddenly appearing in the doorway behind Grace. His face fell when he saw it was me at the door.

'Hey, Olly!' I said, attempting to be as cheery as possible.

'Flick bought me a tortoise, but it's actually a turtle.'

'Oh,' he said, peering into the tank. 'Didn't you work that out from the fact it's in water?'

'How was I supposed to know the distinction? Argh, now his name is stupid.'

'I like him.' Grace smiled, looking happily at her turtle. 'Do you want to come in?'

I sheepishly followed her through into their sitting room and sat down awkwardly on a sofa opposite them.

'Thanks for the turtle,' Grace said. 'I've actually always wanted a terrapin.'

'Oh. Good,' I said. 'It's the least I could do. I wanted to say sorry . . . for being distant.'

'That's OK. I know you've been busy filming.'

'Yeah, look, about that. I've been selfish about the

whole thing and maybe got a bit carried away. Well, I hope you know already . . . but just in case it hasn't been obvious recently, your friendship is way more important to me than a stupid TV show. I was only trying to prove that I wasn't the person Nancy Rose made me out to be after handbag-gate.'

'We know that,' Grace said kindly. 'And the show is a great opportunity, I think it's good that you've been so dedicated. It's important to make sure you feel better about all those Nancy Rose vlogs.'

'I actually realised that I care way more about what you guys think of me than what Nancy Rose or the general public think,' I said firmly.

Grace smiled and I turned to Olly.

'I'm *so* sorry about the gig, Olly. That wasn't meant to happen. All I wanted was to be there, cheering you on, and I told them specifically that I didn't want any cameras.' I sighed. 'I'm so sorry it disrupted your performance and ruined everything. And I hope you and the rest of the band can forgive me.'

He brought his eyes up to meet mine and I swallowed the lump in my throat.

'Grace told me that it wasn't your fault the cameras turned up,' he said, watching me intensely. 'But why didn't you call the next day? I haven't heard from you at all.'

I realised immediately from his expression that he wasn't angry. He was hurt.

'I was too embarrassed. I thought you'd be so cross with me, because you'd have every right to be, and I didn't want to make it all worse. But I haven't stopped thinking about it. And I think I may have a way of making it up to you. If you'll let me.'

He raised his eyebrows.

'It's part of a bigger plan of mine, actually, to right a few wrongs,' I explained. 'It's to do with the ball I'm throwing, which I hope you both still plan to come to. But I completely understand if you're upset with me and don't want to be involved in the ball or anything to do with me. If you need space, I can leave.'

He shared a look with Grace and then, as his mouth curled into a smile, a surge of warmth waved over me and the dread I'd felt at the idea of losing Olly as a friend began to fade.

'No, I don't need space from you, Flick. I've had enough of that recently,' he said, holding my gaze. 'Whatever it is that you've got up your sleeve, I'm in.'

I breathed a sigh of relief. 'Good. That's really good. Then I want to formally invite you to the Hotel Royale for lunch today so I can fill you both in on the plan.'

'Sounds good. Is Cal coming?' Grace asked.

'Um . . .' I looked down at my hands. 'I haven't spoken to him yet. Matthew told me he's got a family thing today. I'm not sure he's still planning on coming to the ball either. He looked really angry at the gig.' My heart sank as I remembered his furious expression right before the sound boom loomed towards him. 'Maybe if I invite Ella to the ball, he'll be more inclined to come.'

'He knows what happened at the gig wasn't your fault,' Grace told me. 'Just like we did. You should message him. And maybe buy him a turtle.'

I smiled. 'It's the best way to earn forgiveness. Anyway, ready to go eat? I'm starving and I know Chef was whipping up some chocolate mousse this morning, so the menu today is looking good.'

'Before we get to the hotel, Flick, I have to tell you something,' Grace said, her expression serious. 'I've been doing some investigating recently —'

'Yeah, Olly said you were working on a mysterious project,' I replied, catching Olly's eye.

'Are you finally going to tell us what you've been up to?' Olly asked hopefully.

Grace nodded. 'I figured it was important to you, Flick, to know the truth.'

'The truth about what?'

She took a deep breath.

'I know who Nancy Rose's source is,' she said. 'And it's not who you think.'

> You know what's funny?
> People keep telling me to message you.
> First it was Audrey and Matthew,
> and now it's Grace. You must talk
> about me a lot when I'm not around, huh?

Hi Flick

> Hi Cal. Anyway, I wanted to tell you
> about some browsing I've just done online.
> You want to know what I found out?

Go on . . .

> Flick Sprogg does exist!!
> Weirdly, she's 74
> and lives in Ohio. I have
> her Facebook page if you
> want to check it's her?

I'll think about it

Am I going to see you
at the charity ball I'm hosting?
You know, the big finale for my show?
Did you know I was doing a show?
I haven't talked about it much

Ha ha. Thanks but I don't think I will.
The whole being on camera stuff isn't
really up my street. Have fun, though!

Now, Callum, I know you're lying
because your dad already let slip
that you were looking for your
bow tie this morning. Apparently,
you said to him it was "just in case"

That was for another thing

Oh really?

Yep

Another black-tie thing?

That's right

What other black-tie thing is it?

It's a ball

Wow! Who is throwing this other black-tie ball?

This guy I know

Hey! I think I know him!

OK, OK, OK. There's not another ball

NO WAY!

But this doesn't mean I'm coming to yours

Not even in the knowledge that Ella is coming?

You invited Ella? I don't believe you

Ask her. We just got off the phone. You know, if your whole editorial team is going to be there, you probably should make an appearance

I suppose it would be irresponsible not to. Thanks, Flick

Good. Also, I'm sorry. About the gig. And about other stuff

You've always had such a beautiful way with words

Flick Sprogg doesn't live in Ohio

I know

She isn't 74, either

I know that too

She lives in London and, judging by her Instagram, she's pretty awesome at Lego building

Stop stalking her

I am NOT stalking her. But seriously, the castle she built in 2014 was very impressive. Have you seen it? You must have seen it. Because you're such close friends

No. I haven't spoken to her in years. We're not friends

HA! In your face, Flick Sprogg! There's only one Flick in this town

Night, Flick xx

Do you think, if I asked, she could build me a Lego dragon?

TWENTY-THREE

'Are you ready?' Mum asked.

'I think so,' I said nervously, glancing around the packed ballroom. 'Although, I'm so nervous, I feel a bit sick. I wish someone else could do the speech for me while I go and hide somewhere, and then I could come out when everything is sorted.'

'Where would the fun be in that?' Mum smiled. 'And besides, no one wearing a dress like that should feel the need to go and hide.'

I had to admit that Lewis Blume had really outdone himself with my dress for the ball. 'It must be even more striking than the one I designed for your Christmas ball,' he had declared as I'd explained the situation and what I had in store for the evening. 'You leave it with me!'

Whereas at Christmas I'd worn emerald green, this time he'd dressed me in a beautiful deep royal blue. It was covered in hand-embroidered beads from the high neckline down to the delicate beaded waistband, with a full satin sweep-train skirt. The hotel beautician, Danielle, had said that I looked like I'd stepped out of *A Midsummer Night's Dream*, so I decided to style my hair to match that theme, plaiting it in a very pretty halo braid.

Almost all the guests had now arrived for the ball and were enjoying an amazing performance by Sky, who was singing some songs from her latest album, accompanied by a pianist. Prince Gustav was standing right in front of the temporary stage we'd had built in the ballroom for the occasion, swaying along to her songs, gazing up at her dreamily and ignoring any guest that came over to talk to him.

Sky had met up with him that morning and it turned out that he didn't want to break up with her at all. He was so in love with her that he'd been scared she'd forget all about him after a while back in LA.

'He decided to handle it by distancing himself, so he wouldn't get hurt when I called it off,' Sky had told me as we got ready together earlier. 'I told him I was in it for the long run, if he was.'

'And?' I'd asked, as her eyes went all misty and she got this dopey smile on her face.

'*And* he asked me to move in with him. He just got a place here in London.'

'AND?' I'd asked, my jaw dropping to the floor. 'WHAT WAS YOUR ANSWER?'

'Duh!' She'd laughed at the sight of my expression. 'I said yes.'

My voice was now VERY hoarse from all the excited squealing that had exploded at that point.

Mum, Fritz and I had been at the door of the ballroom all evening, greeting guests as they trickled in. Fritz looked especially handsome in the matching royal-blue tuxedo Lewis Blume had designed for him, although he found greeting guests particularly tiresome and was now reclining on one of his plush velvet cushions with his tongue lolling out, having his tummy tickled by the president of France.

'The evening has gone perfectly so far,' Mum said, taking it all in. Her eyes lingered on the camera crew being directed by Francine and Hazel in the far corner. Hazel was excitedly pointing out the most famous guests, instructing the cameras to get them in shot.

'So,' Mum continued, tearing her gaze from Hazel practically dragging the recent winner of *Strictly Come Dancing* in front of a camera lens, 'when are you going up on stage?'

'After Sky's set,' I told her, grinning as I saw Olly, Grace, Ella and Cal coming down the corridor towards the ballroom. 'Everyone is here now.'

I left Mum at the door of the ballroom to chat with a

celebrity chef who came over to her, and rushed to give Grace a big hug. She looked very pretty in a turquoise prom dress with a sparkling silver clutch.

'You look amazing!'

'Thanks,' she said, 'I decided my dress should be a sea-like colour in honour of Tortoise.'

'You mean the turtle,' I corrected.

'No, I mean Tortoise. I kept the name. I think it has a ring to it.'

I laughed and then turned to Olly. He looked so good in his black tie that I found myself blushing when he leaned in to give me a kiss on the cheek.

'Hey,' he said with a smile, pulling away. 'Everything is ready when you are. Just let me know when you want it all set up.'

'I will,' I replied, my hands beginning to tingle with nerves as Sky announced into the microphone that she was about to sing her last song of the evening.

'Thanks for this,' Olly said.

'Honestly, it's the least I could do,' I replied, looking up at him and then finding myself in a bit of a daze.

His eyes are so prettyyyyyyyyyy. They are literally as mesmerising as Ethan Duke's jaw.

'Eyes,' I said.

He blinked. 'Huh?'

OH MY GOD I JUST SAID EYES FOR NO REASON.

OK, seriously, why can't I appreciate other people's beautiful features without saying those features OUT LOUD?

'Uh . . . I said *nice*. Nice evening. This is a nice evening. Anyway,' I said, clearing my throat, 'you should probably go and get everything ready to go.'

'All right, then,' he agreed excitedly. 'I'll see you all in a bit.'

As he disappeared into the crowd, Ella's voice rang out from behind where he'd been standing.

'What is in this? Raspberry?' she asked, examining the pink mocktail Timothy had offered her. It matched her pale pink gown.

'Yeah,' I replied, moving around Olly to stand in front of her, pleased to be out from under the spell of his ridiculous eyes. 'Jamie, our sommelier, came up with that concoction. Do you like it?'

'It's not bad.'

I took a deep breath. 'I owe you an apology, Ella. I know it wasn't you who was leaking those stories about me to Nancy Rose. I'm sorry for accusing you.'

She hesitated, watching me thoughtfully as though weighing up whether to accept my apology or not.

'Well,' she said, eventually, 'maybe in the future, you

should make sure you have your facts straight.'

'I'll make sure of that.'

She nodded.

'And I suppoooooose,' she said in a quieter voice, rolling her eyes as though reluctant to say the rest of her sentence out loud, 'I shouldn't have called you a diva in front of those cameras.'

I smiled warmly at her. 'Thanks. I appreciate that.'

'I'm going to go get another of these raspberry things,' she announced, craning her neck to look over my shoulder.

I moved aside to let her pass, leaving Cal the last one left to greet.

'Hey,' he said, moving closer. 'Nice dress.'

'You found your bow tie.'

'Well, I needed it for the other ball thrown by that guy,' he said, grinning. 'So, it was lying around.'

I stood there awkwardly, not knowing whether to give him a hug or a kiss on the cheek or something. I mean, it's CAL and I see him pretty much every day, lingering around the hotel or at school, so giving him a hug hello every time would be weird, but then at the same time, at these kind of events you're meant to greet your guests with *something*.

WHAT DO I DO? WHY ISN'T THERE SOME KIND OF GUIDE BOOK FOR THIS?

OK, Olly had given me a kiss on the cheek and that was nice, so I figured I should go for something similar with Cal and, quite frankly, ANYTHING was better than the two of us just awkwardly standing in front of each other.

I took a step towards him but someone grabbed my arm, and I spun round to see Hazel beaming at me.

'Tonight is going VERY well,' she informed me, checking that my hair was perfectly in place. 'All the right people are here. This is just the kind of interest we need for the show to be a big hit. Francine was telling me it's the perfect finale for the pilot, just the sort of *pizzazz* she was after.'

'I'm glad you're having a nice time,' I replied, glancing up at the stage as Sky finished her song and took a bow.

'You could look a little more excited, Flick! This is all for you, you know.' She beamed, gesturing around the ballroom.

'Is it?' I asked, watching her closely, but she didn't seem to notice my question.

'What a party. Ah, Tanya is waving at me,' she said, giving her a nod. 'I'll come find you later, darling.'

She swanned past me, towards Tanya in the middle of the crowd.

On the other side of the room, Sky caught my eye and gave me a thumbs up. I turned to Cal and Grace.

'OK, I'm on,' I said, swallowing the lump in my throat. 'Wish me luck.'

'Good luck!' Grace squeaked as Cal stood with a bemused expression.

I made my way to the performance space, taking the microphone from its stand and tapping it lightly to check that it was still on.

'Good evening,' I announced, shuddering with a wave of nerves as the sea of faces turned in my direction. 'I'm Flick Royale. Thank you for being here tonight.'

Francine's face popped up above the crowd as she gestured wildly for the cameras to focus on me and two sound booms appeared above my head.

'As you all know, your donations this evening are for charity and I'm happy to announce that all the money raised tonight will be going to a brand-new charity that I am very proud to have launched.'

I could see Hazel was stunned, but pretending not to be. This was all news to her.

'And that charity is . . . Fritz's Faithful Friends! Funding assistance and therapy dogs across Britain!'

There was a loud round of applause and, as instructed, Timothy lifted Fritz into the air on his cushion. Observing his adoring audience from his cushioned throne, Fritz looked very pleased with himself.

'That is what this ball tonight is all about,' I continued. 'And some of you may have noticed the cameras around the room. As you may know, it has recently been reported in the press that I am filming a pilot episode for my own reality TV series . . .'

My eyes flickered towards Hazel. She was whispering in Tanya's ear smugly.

It was now or never.

'But,' I said, determinedly, 'I can tell you now that those reports are wrong. There will be no reality TV show about me.'

Hazel stopped whispering.

'You see,' I continued, 'I realised something recently. I was making so much effort and spending so much time trying to *look* like a good person, that I began to forget what it means to *be* one. I was trying to be the "real me" and forgot to just be . . . me.'

I could see Mum at the back of the room beaming at me, her eyes glistening.

'That's why I've decided that, instead of doing a reality show, I will actually be hosting a big auction next week here at Hotel Royale of all the beautiful items I've been kindly given for taking part in a reality series – beautiful clothes, shoes, beauty products, event tickets, VIP passes – to raise money for Fritz's Faithful Friends.

239

Everyone is welcome.'

As the room erupted into applause again, Hazel looked as though someone had slapped her across the face. The crew were all looking in confusion at Francine, whose mouth was slack.

'So, without further ado now that that's over, I would like to introduce a very special emerging band to play for you all.' I smiled and gestured to the group edging towards the performance space. 'Olly, take it away.'

★ TWENTY-FOUR ❀

'How could you do this?' Hazel cried, as I led her away from the ballroom and into the empty music room so we could be alone. 'After everything we've worked so hard for?'

I shut the door behind me.

'Hazel, I know it was you leaking those stories to Nancy Rose.'

She froze.

'What?' she whimpered. 'What are you —'

'My friend Grace found out. She's devoted a lot of her time recently to this secret investigative project and, it turns out, she wanted to find out the truth about who told Nancy Rose about my incident with Prince Gustav last year, the peacock thing, and then who filled her in about the reality TV show. Grace knew I was upset about it and, being the most incredible friend that she is, plus the smartest student in school, she set to work tracking down Nancy Rose's "source". And it turns out it was you.'

Hazel sat down slowly into an armchair. I sat in the one opposite.

'Flick,' she said timidly, 'you have to know I had your best interests at heart. I didn't plan on any of this. But when you were suddenly thrown into the public eye because of your scuffle with Nancy Rose, I couldn't bear the idea of you fading away simply because you didn't know how to harness the attention properly. You see, you're in a wonderful position as the heiress to Hotel Royale. I didn't want you to waste it.' She paused. 'I never had that opportunity and I didn't want you to get brushed aside, like I was.'

'What do you mean brushed aside?' I asked. 'By Mum?'

'By everyone. Don't get me wrong, I had no interest in running the family business,' she admitted, leaning back. 'It was always public knowledge that Christine was going to take over. She was the one with the business mind and passion for the hotel. But because of that, no one had the slightest bit of interest in me. I was never even considered for the "50 Heirs to Watch" list.'

'But when I was dropped from that list, you told Nancy Rose that it was time everyone saw the "real me".'

'Yes! I meant that positively,' she insisted. 'The *real* Flick Royale, I told her, was going to be a big star. I got on the first flight from New York. I wanted you to seize the moment! That's why I fed Nancy Rose some . . . harmless insights into your life. Just to make sure she kept talking about you. And then the reality TV show opportunity fell into our laps and your future became very bright indeed.'

'Nancy Rose made me out to be a diva who ATTACKED royalty!'

'Yes, well,' she said with a sniff, 'that Nancy Rose certainly used her artistic licence when it came to her portrayal of what I'd told her. I absolutely never said you attacked anyone. Flick –' she looked me straight in the eye – 'I won't deny that I contacted her, but I only told her the truth about those incidents and then she twisted them, I swear.'

I didn't say anything.

'I only wanted to help your career,' she continued, leaning forwards and holding my gaze. 'I'm so sorry if I hurt your feelings. I knew I had to keep the buzz about you high. You have no idea how easy it is to fade into the distance and how quickly you can be forgotten. I knew you'd had a go at vlogging, and it hadn't been too successful, so I thought the TV show would be something that you'd want.' She let out a long sigh. 'I admit that I may have let my own ambitions for you cloud my judgement; I got carried away and for that I am truly sorry. But I just wanted to help you.'

I still didn't say anything, letting her words sink in.

'OK,' I said, eventually. 'I understand why you did it.

And I got carried away too, so I get it. But I think for now I need a break from the public eye. I'm kind of OK with fading away.'

She smiled weakly. 'At least you know where to find me if ever you need an agent.' She reached out and took my hand in hers. 'You're a very special girl, Flick. You may have the sense of your mother, but I like to think your star quality comes from me.'

I laughed as the door to the music room opened and Mum popped her head round.

'There you are!' she said. 'Everyone's looking for you!'

Hazel quickly leaned close to me and whispered, 'Have you told your mother about me and Nancy Rose yet?'

'Nope. I thought I'd leave that honour to you.'

'Any chance I can tell her on the phone once I'm safely back in New York?'

'I've learned that it's better to face your problems and admit when you're wrong,' I said encouragingly. 'You want me to stay with you?'

Hazel sighed, slowly shaking her head. 'No. Go and enjoy your party, you deserve it. I'll handle Christine.' She gave me a small smile. 'She still owes me for the time she blamed me for smashing Mum's vase. If she gets too mad, I may have to slide that into the conversation.'

'What's going on?' Mum asked, approaching us.

'Hazel, I know you'll be disappointed about the television show but Flick is really grateful for all your help with it anyway.'

'Christine,' Hazel said, gesturing for Mum to take my place, 'you should probably sit down.'

'Don't be angry for too long,' I told Mum, as I stood up to leave. 'I've already made a reservation for us three to have breakfast in the morning. I think it's about time the Royale women sat down and talked about things other than business, don't you?'

★ ❀ �

I went back into the ballroom and was engulfed in a hug from Grace right away.

'You did it!' she cried. 'How do you feel?'

'Like a big weight has been lifted from my shoulders,' I said, smiling. 'And like I've finally done the right thing.'

'To be honest, I'm a bit disappointed that I won't be able to see the cupcake saga on national television. My hair looked very good that day,' she said, winking at me. 'Scene-stealing, one might say.'

I laughed before glancing nervously at Francine and Tanya, who had left the ballroom to stand in the corridor and talk frantically into their phones.

'They haven't put their phones down since your announcement,' Grace informed me. 'The camera crew seemed a bit lost as to what to do so, while you were with Hazel, Audrey ushered them out and took them down to the kitchen to sample some of Chef's new chocolate mousse.'

'Well, hopefully that should make up a little bit for me wasting so much of their time.'

'I wouldn't worry too much,' Grace said. 'I overheard Francine telling whoever she's speaking to that your change of heart has freed up her schedule, so she can pitch a new project about some princess she's been thinking about. I think the princess is a distant cousin of Prince Gustav.'

I laughed, watching Prince Gustav twirl Sky around to Olly's song. As all the guests began to join in dancing to the band's performance, I beamed up at Olly proudly.

'He's not bad, is he?' Grace said, following my gaze. 'I hope this little moment in the spotlight doesn't make his head any bigger than it already is. I had better go and get a good spot up front so I can send a video to Mum and Dad.'

'Sky and Prince Gustav are right by the stage,' I pointed out. 'They've got a good view there.'

'Maybe Sky will let me get another selfie with her,' she

enthused, before giving me another hug. 'Well done again for this evening, Flick. As excited as I was to have a best friend with her own reality TV show and millions of fans, I think I prefer having you all to myself.'

I laughed again as she excitedly scampered off into the crowd, and then I turned when I felt a tap on my shoulder.

'So, the reality TV world isn't for you after all, then?' Cal asked, handing me a pink mocktail.

I clinked his glass with mine. 'Fritz and I decided that our talents lay elsewhere.'

He nodded, watching me carefully. 'Are you OK? I know how excited you were about having your own show and everything that came with it.'

'Yeah, well, it turns out having your own show is overrated I'm happy being off-camera.' I smiled. 'Although, having my own perfume range would have been pretty awesome.'

Cal grinned. 'Can't say I'll miss the sound guy swinging that boom mic around and nearly knocking my head off with it.'

'And I won't miss Francine instructing me to be more dramatic with the way I sip my coffee in the mornings,' I said, rolling my eyes and making him chuckle.

I paused, reluctant to say what I had to next. Saying

things out loud always seems to make them more real. But last night, lying in bed, I'd realised that I needed to finally accept Ella, if that's what Cal wanted, otherwise I really would lose him.

'Cal,' I said as he took a sip of his mocktail, 'I really hope that you can forgive me for assuming Ella was the one telling Nancy Rose stories about me. I don't want you to think I can't hang out with your . . . girlfriend.'

He suddenly began choking on his drink, so I clapped him hard on the back.

'Sorry,' he spluttered, wiping his mouth with his sleeve. 'Did you just say . . . *girlfriend*?'

'Yeah,' I said as enthusiastically as possible. 'I know you have got close and I don't want you thinking that I . . .'

My sentence fizzled out as Cal burst out laughing.

Which, you know, made me a little bit annoyed because I was trying to make amends and he wasn't being very kind about it by laughing in my face.

'I'm sorry,' he wheezed, noticing my expression. 'I just . . . you think *Ella* is my *girlfriend*?'

'Well, yeah,' I said, furrowing my brow in confusion, 'you are always together at school —'

'For the paper,' he said, looking at me as though I was mad. 'She's trying to get an internship at a fashion magazine for the spring holiday, remember? She's been trying to contribute to the paper as much as possible. It will look good for her internship application, that's all.'

'But . . . but then she came along as your date to the gig . . .'

'My *date*? No, Flick, I invited her because we were all talking about the gig in the editorial meeting and I thought it would be a bit rude to talk about it in front of her and not invite her. I was actually quite surprised when she said yes, but then Olly mentioned how she had been messaging Harry recently and it all made a lot more sense.'

'Harry?' I looked towards the stage. 'The drummer in Olly's band?'

'Yeah, apparently there's a spark there.' He grinned, shaking his head at me. 'Anyway, I can safely assure you that Ella is NOT my girlfriend. She's not really my type. Too much hair flicking.'

'Oh! Right. Cool!'

We stood together for a bit, watching Olly's band play, not saying anything. I tried to act normal but I couldn't stop smiling. A warm tingly feeling had washed over me at the news that, even though we'd come to a truce, Ella would not be a permanent fixture of our group.

After a few minutes, Cal caught me glancing up at him and he smiled.

'Flick,' he said, 'can I ask you something?'

'Sure!' I hesitated. 'Although, wait, is this about your green jumper? Because if so, you don't need to ask . . . yes, I'm going to get it dry-cleaned. I know it's not ideal, but to be honest it's no wonder Fritz mistook it for a toilet when you left it all crumpled up behind reception. It looked a bit like grass so you can see how he got confused.'

'Wait, WHAT?'

'Oh! Matthew didn't tell you?'

'Which jumper? What do you mean Fritz mistook it for a TOILET?'

'Never mind! What was it you wanted to ask me?'

He narrowed his eyes at Fritz sitting nearby before returning his attention to me.

'I was going to ask if you'd let me report on what happened tonight for the school newspaper. I finally found the front-page story I was hoping for.'

I blinked up at him. 'You want to write a story about this? Seriously?'

'Yeah, I do. What do you reckon?'

'I don't know. I mean, is it good enough for a front page? What exactly would you say?'

'Well, this story has got everything,' he pointed out. 'Fame, friends, drama, scandal, and an unexpected twist.'

'You're right.' I nodded. 'But you've forgotten the most important thing.'

'Oh yeah?' He grinned, his eyes twinkling. 'What's that?'

'Isn't it obvious?' I asked, my heart bursting at the sight of those familiar dimples. 'A happy ending.'

ACKNOWLEDGEMENTS

Huge thanks to Lindsey Heaven, Emily Sharratt, Alice Hill, Siobhan McDermott and the talented Egmont family for all your support and guidance. I am so grateful to you for your hard work and for making me look much better than I actually am.

Special thanks to the remarkable wonder that is my friend and agent, Lauren Gardner. Without your encouragement, none of this would be possible. I really am very lucky to have you in my corner.

To my wonderful family and friends, thank you for always cheering me on and making me laugh every day. Seriously, thanks for being so weird and hilarious in your own unique ways. I'm stealing all your genius and putting it in books. Keep it coming.

My Labradors continue to provide inspiration for my writing, including the misadventures of Fritz, and for that I owe them big time, so Dougal, Archie and Lara: I hereby promise to keep sneaking you biscuits and letting you up on the sofa (sorry Dad, my hands are tied).

And to all my readers, thank you for picking up my books and accompanying me on all these adventures. Here's to our next one.

MORE HILARIOUS ANTICS FROM KATY BIRCHALL IN *the it girl* SERIES

Read on a for a sneak peek of book 1...

EVERYONE WANTS TO BE FAMOUS. DON'T THEY?

the it girl

SUPERSTAR GEEK

KATY BIRCHALL

I set Josie Graham on fire.

And, OK, yes it was bad but it was an accident and not *entirely* my fault. Everyone thinks I did it on purpose. They think Mrs Ginnwell is a hero.

If you ask me, Mrs Ginnwell made the whole thing worse. A little bit of water would have sorted everything out just fine. It was only the ends of her hair and a fire extinguisher was a very dramatic plan of action. I mean, Josie was already having a pretty bad day considering I'd just set her on fire and everything, and the next thing she knew she was covered head to toe in that white foamy stuff that always looks like it might be fun to play in but probably isn't. (I think Josie looked more in shock – and a little bit itchy – than like she was having fun.)

I was kind of in shock myself. I'd never set fire to anyone before so the whole incident came as a bit of a surprise. The closest I've been to any kind of arson was when I was little and I put my dad's wallet on the log fire to see what would happen. I mean, who leaves their wallet laying around in the same room as a toddler? Not my father any more that's for sure. But I still think he looks at me a little bit suspiciously on cold nights.

Oh, and there *was* that time I almost burnt down Dad's study. But those two times are IT.

And you know what? This is partly Josie Graham's fault too. Because really, she should not have been (a) leaning on her hand so close to a Bunsen burner and (b) wearing so much hairspray to school.

I'm just jealous because I don't have the time, let alone the skills, for hairspray. Once Dad has eventually wrestled the duvet cover away from me, I have about ten minutes tops to get ready.

My dad would never buy me hairspray anyway. He's so old fashioned, especially when it comes to his fourteen-year-old daughter. I remember one time in a pharmacy I asked him if he would buy me eyeliner. He burst out laughing and made me go fetch some Lemsip. I think this is VERY hypocritical as some of the women my dad has dated have worn a LOT of dark eyeliner. How would he feel if, when he introduced them, I laughed in their face and gave them a mug of hot lemon paracetamol instead?

Hmm . . . I might consider this for the really annoying ones that get brought home.

A wobbling Mrs Ginnwell definitely wasn't laughing

as she marched me into Miss Duke's office mumbling something incoherent about fire in the classroom and pyromaniac tendencies.

'Sorry, Mrs Ginnwell, I didn't quite understand that. What did you say?' Miss Duke asked, rising from her desk with a look of concern.

Miss Duke really suits her office. Which sounds strange when I say it out loud but it just goes with her overall vibe. She's new to the school too. We were both new in September, although obviously she's a bit more senior being headmistress and everything. I just came into Year 10. Everything considered, I think she has managed to set the better impression out of the two of us so far. This is not great considering she gives out detentions and makes people pick up rubbish from behind the bike shed.

So even though she's only been in that office for a term and I'm not entirely sure what it looked like before she arrived, it matches her. For example, it's all very neat. Miss Duke is very formal and smartly dressed. She looks more like those businesswomen who are always on their hands-free mobiles in train stations barking things like, 'That's just damn well not good enough, Jeffrey,' than a headmistress at a co-ed school.

I like the way she can pull off a trouser suit though. I think if ever I was going to work in an office I would like to wear a trouser suit and look authoritative like Miss Duke does. And her dark hair is always so neatly pinned and her make-up never smudged. She is very intimidating.

Even more so when you've just set your classmate's hair on fire.

'Chemistry class . . . Anna . . . Anna set . . . hair . . . Josie Graham on fire!' Mrs Ginnwell finally spluttered.

Mrs Ginnwell is neither authoritative nor intimidating. She kind of reminds me of a parrot. But not a cool one that would chill with a pirate. An overzealous one that swoops around your head, squawking and whacking you unexpectedly in the face with its wings.

'Is Josie all right?' Miss Duke asked in alarm.

Mrs Ginnwell nodded, her curled strawberry blonde hair frizzing around her sweaty forehead. 'Fine. Although her hair is quite singed and covered in foam.'

'I see,' Miss Duke replied and I swear I saw her smirk for a second. If she did it was gone in an instant when she caught my eye. 'And no one else was hurt in this incident?'

'No.' Mrs Ginwell shook her head.

'Well in that case, Anna, you can have a seat and, Jenny, why don't you pop into the teachers' lounge and ask someone to cover your lesson for a bit while you get a cup of tea.'

Mrs Ginnwell nodded and slowly released her grip

on me. She gave me a very pointed look, as if when let loose I would pull out a flamethrower from my locker and burn the school to the ground. Which is a completely ridiculous thought for her to entertain because last term I did an excellent essay on penguins. No one who puts that much effort and emotional maturity into a Year 10 essay about penguins would be spending their free time plotting to destroy their school.

I sat down slowly into the leather chair opposite Miss Duke, who was settling into her chair behind the desk. The heavy wooden door closed loudly as Mrs Ginnwell escaped, still glaring at me, and there was a moment of silence as Miss Duke straightened the forms she had been filling in before we interrupted her afternoon.

'So, why don't you explain to me exactly what happened?'

I took a deep breath and told her how we had been in our Chemistry lesson and Josie and I had been partnered together, which, by the way, neither of us were too happy about. I didn't tell Miss Duke that part though.

I assumed she would know that it had been an unhappy arrangement. Josie is one of the most popular girls in our year. She's best friends with Queen Bee, Sophie Parker, and they're always hanging out with the popular boys in our year like Brendan Dakers and James Tyndale. Josie spends her weekends partying and comes to school wearing a full face of make-up and her hair sprayed perfectly into place.

I spend my weekends reading comics, watching *CSI* with my dad and complaining about my life to my yellow Labrador, called Dog, who is the only creature on this planet who listens to me. And I can only get him to listen if I'm holding a bit of bacon.

So I skipped out the part of the story where Josie looked miserably at Brendan, who she was clearly hoping to be partnered with, and then came to sit next to me with a big sigh and no greeting. She didn't even look at me when I went, 'Howdy, partner,' in a courageous attempt to lighten the atmosphere.

I really don't know why that was the greeting I went with.

She couldn't be bothered to do the experiment so I just got on with it. Now, technically, Mrs Ginnwell had not explained the Bunsen burner part of the experiment yet as everyone was putting on their lab coats and goggles. But some people were taking their time and Josie, leaning on her hand, kept glancing at Brendan, laughing at whatever he was saying to her and flicking her hair dramatically.

I guess this is where it kind of becomes my fault. I should have waited until we were told to start up the

Bunsen burners but I went ahead and turned ours on.

There are a few very important things to remember here:

1. I did not realise it was on the highest flame setting.

2. I did not realise that, just as I turned it on, Josie would flick her hairspray-laden locks in the direction that she did.

3. I did not realise that her hair was quite so flammable.

4. I did not realise that she would run around screaming rather than stay still so that throwing water at her became increasingly difficult and my aim isn't that good anyway so I actually ended up just soaking myself.

5. I did not expect Mrs Ginnwell to use so much foam that Josie resembled a poodle.

6. It should also be remembered that I have never been in any real trouble at school before this incident.

7. Apart from that time when I was six and Ben Metton ate my Hula Hoops so I locked him in the stationery cupboard.

8. The whole fire incident is in fact very upsetting

for me too as I didn't mean to do it, I feel awful and now no one will want to stay friends with me, just like at my last school.

At this point I started crying.

Miss Duke, who had been staring at me in shock, passed me a tissue. 'Well, it sounds to me like it was an accident –' she began.

'Of course it was an accident!' I wailed, interrupting her. 'I would never do that on purpose!'

There was a knock on the door and I turned in my seat to see the school nurse slowly pop her head round. Miss Duke beckoned her in and she came forward happily. 'I wanted to let you know, Miss Duke, and you, Anna, that Josie is perfectly fine. Her hair is singed at the end and she'll have to have a haircut but apart from that she is right as rain.'

'She must hate me,' I said glumly, staring at the damp, crumpled tissue in my hand.

'I'm sure she doesn't. She'll get over it,' the nurse said jovially. 'Her hair was so long and straggly anyway – a cut will probably improve things.'

'Er, *thank* you, Tricia,' Miss Duke said pointedly. The nurse gave a cheerful shrug and left.

'There you go, that's something,' Miss Duke

announced. 'It was clearly an accident but one that could have had nasty consequences. We've been lucky, Anna.'

I nodded gravely.

'I hope that from now on you won't begin any kind of experiment without instruction.'

'I'm never going to do another experiment again.'

'I hope you will. Chemistry is a fascinating subject and I imagine you've learnt an important lesson with regards to safety.' She looked at me sternly. 'Right, well, while we've established this wasn't intentional, I'm going to have to give you detention lasting the remainder of this term so that you can reflect on the importance of caution. It starts tomorrow. And since it is the end of the day in about ten minutes, you can return to your classroom, gather your things and go home.'

'I'd rather not go back, to be honest.'

'You don't need anything?'

'It's just my pencil case and books. People have probably thrown them in the dump by now.'

'I'm sure that's not true.' Miss Duke gave a thin smile. 'They all know it was an accident and no harm done. By tomorrow they'll have forgotten the whole thing.'

It's worrying how clueless adults are sometimes.